"Something's not right."

Simone put her hand on her weapon beneath her jacket.

Ian reached to pull her farther away from the entrance just as the crack of a rifle echoed through the air. The glass door in front of Ian burst into a million pieces. The swirl of air as the bullet zinged close to his head jolted him into action. He instinctively turned away from the spray of glass and grabbed for Simone, intending to pull her out of the line of fire.

Her hands wrapped around his biceps and she launched him to the ground, her body draping over him. He struggled against her, wanting to reverse their positions so that he could shield her. He wasn't going to let her take a bullet for him. More bullets hit the entryway. Close. A shudder of fear racked him.

They were pinned down. An assassin wanted Ian dead at any cost, and Ian feared his bodyguards were going to be the ones to pay the ultimate price. No way could he allow that.

Terri Reed's romance and romantic suspense novels have appeared on the *Publishers Weekly* top twenty-five and Nielsen BookScan top one hundred lists, and have been featured in *USA TODAY*, *Christian Fiction* magazine and *RT Book Reviews*. Her books have been finalists for the Romance Writers of America RITA® Award and the National Readers' Choice Award and finalists three times for the American Christian Fiction Writers Carol Award. Contact Terri at terrireed.com or PO Box 19555, Portland, OR 97224.

Books by Terri Reed

Love Inspired Suspense

Buried Mountain Secrets
Secret Mountain Hideout
Christmas Protection Detail
Secret Sabotage

Alaska K-9 Unit

Alaskan Rescue

True Blue K-9 Unit: Brooklyn

Explosive Situation

True Blue K-9 Unit

Seeking the Truth

Military K-9 Unit

Tracking Danger
Mission to Protect

Visit the Author Profile page at LoveInspired.com for more titles.

SECRET SABOTAGE

TERRI REED

LOVE INSPIRED SUSPENSE

INSPIRATIONAL ROMANCE

LOVE INSPIRED® SUSPENSE
INSPIRATIONAL ROMANCE

ISBN-13: 978-1-335-55480-2

Recycling programs
for this product may
not exist in your area.

Secret Sabotage

This edition published by arrangement with Harlequin Books S.A.

For questions and comments about the quality of this book, please contact us at CustomerService@Harlequin.com.

Love Inspired
22 Adelaide St. West, 41st Floor
Toronto, Ontario M5H 4E3, Canada
www.LoveInspired.com

Printed in U.S.A.

There is no fear in love; but perfect love casteth out fear: because fear hath torment. He that feareth is not made perfect in love.
—*1 John* 4:18

To all the women and men who have been on the front lines of every battle in 2020. May God shine His face upon you and yours and heap blessings upon you.

To my editors, Emily Rodmell and Tina James, for your infinite patience and support.

ONE

"Mayday, mayday!" Ian Delaney shouted into the microphone on his headset, his voice cracking with adrenaline.

Determined not to give in to the jolt of fear coursing through his body, he worked the controls. The engine sputtered, sending a vibration through the helicopter so strong his teeth rattled. He prayed the air traffic controller manning the small airport atop the mountain outside of Bristle Township, Colorado, received his distress call.

Dread swamped him, filling his veins. He deployed the emergency beacon that would send out his GPS location on the backside of the mountain and gripped the cyclic pitch lever with all his might in an effort to keep the copter from a downward spiral. His feet worked the pedals to no avail.

He didn't understand how this could be happening. He'd checked and double-checked all the preflight protocols. Clearly, something had gone massively wrong. Intentional sabotage? Because of what he'd discovered?

His heart hammered in his chest. He turned the information he'd uncovered over again in his head for the hundredth time. He should have informed the sheriff and let

Alex look into the mysterious cargo being routed through Bristle Township, but Ian needed to protect his family. What shenanigans was his father up to this time? And if it wasn't his father's doing, then who? What secrets were hidden beneath the forest canopy racing by below?

The helicopter spun, the tail rotor ceasing to keep from balancing the torque. The tall, lush branches of hemlock and pine trees reached up like greedy fingers, eager to pluck him from the autumn sky. The main rotor gave out with a clang and the helicopter took a nosedive into the trees. The loud piercing scream of the warning signal filled his ears.

He braced for impact.

"Please, God, spare me!"

His breath stalled in his throat. A tight vise squeezed his chest. He'd failed his family. Who would protect them now?

The helicopter crashed through the branches, metal twisting and breaking. Ian's head slammed hard against the craft's frame and the world dimmed to nothingness.

This is the man I have to protect.

Simone Walker stared at the bruised and battered man unconscious in the hospital bed. His perfectly sculpted features were marred by a cut over his right eye that had required four stitches. There was swelling everywhere else.

Why had the CEO of Delaney Holdings been flying his helicopter over a mountain in the middle of a Colorado forest?

And who had wanted him dead?

To her, he was just another rich, overindulged man

who'd found himself in trouble. His family had hired her to step in and provide protection. But that was the job.

Working for Trent Associates, a personal protection agency out of Boston, Simone went where the assignment took her. It was up to her to make sure the subject stayed safe. Failure was not an option.

But she had failed in the past. Her gut twisted. The knowledge always lurked in the shadows of her mind, taunting her with the death of a childhood friend and the line she'd almost crossed in the name of revenge.

"Do I know you?"

Simone started at the masculine voice coming from her charge and the strange sort of awareness that shimmied over her. She narrowed her gaze. Apparently, he wasn't unconscious, after all. How long had he been studying her through the slits of his swollen eyelids? Probably as long as she'd been studying him. "You're awake."

He opened his brown eyes fully and winced, half closing his right one. No doubt the stitches pulled. "Where am I?"

"Hospital." She opened the room door and stepped into the doorway to address the deputy sheriff stationed outside. He'd introduced himself earlier as Deputy Chase Fredrick. "He's awake. Get the sheriff and the doctor."

Chase snapped to attention. "I'll let his family know, too."

Simone watched the deputy hurry down the hallway to the nurses' station. Though she wanted to believe that the local law enforcement officers, or LEOs, were on the up-and-up, she couldn't discount anyone from being a suspect in the attempted murder of Ian Delaney, an old habit from her days as a homicide detective for the Detroit police department.

"Excuse me."

Delaney's commanding tone grated on her nerves. She stepped back into the room. "The doctor is coming."

"You didn't answer me," Ian said. "Who are you? Not a nurse. Some sort of law enforcement?"

Hiking an eyebrow, she asked, "How do you figure?"

"Your clothes."

Simone glanced down at her black flats, black two-piece pantsuit and crisp white shirt. She did look like a fed. "Fair enough." She walked to the end of the hospital bed. "My name is Simone Walker. I'm with Trent Associates. Your brother hired me for security."

"I don't understand. Why would I need a bodyguard?"

"Good question. Why don't you tell me?"

"I wouldn't ask the question if I already knew the answer." His voice held a note of exasperation.

In her experience, denial was always the default mode. She didn't believe for a second he had no clue who'd tampered with his helicopter and why. "What kind of trouble are you in?"

Ian's good eye widened. "Trouble? I don't know what you're talking about."

Classic. "What do you know?"

Before he could answer, the door opened and the doctor, a tall, elderly gentleman with salt-and-pepper hair wearing a white lab coat, strode into the room. He was followed by a nurse in green scrubs. Simone moved aside and planted herself where she could watch Ian and keep an eye on the medical professionals.

"Mr. Delaney, I'm Dr. Anders. I'm glad to see you are awake. Your family is on the way." He took out a penlight and checked Ian's pupils. Then he removed the stethoscope from around his neck to listen to Ian's heart.

"What happened to me, Doctor?" Ian asked.

Dr. Anders glanced at Simone.

"We'll wait for the sheriff," she said.

The doctor gave a nod of acknowledgment.

Ian tried to sit up. "I demand to know what's going on."

Of course he did. With his wealth and privilege, Ian Delaney spoke and people jumped. Simone kept her expression even, despite the disdain for the arrogant man souring her stomach.

Dr. Anders put a staying hand on Ian's shoulder. "Settle down there, son. You have multiple contusions but thankfully no broken bones. You have a laceration over your right eye that required sutures. There is some edema, and we're concerned about swelling on your brain. I've ordered a CT scan. Let's get you to Imaging."

Simone held up a hand. "Is this medically necessary at the moment?"

Anders straightened and rolled his shoulders back. "Yes, Miss Walker."

"Then let's go." Simone moved toward the door.

The doctor frowned.

She smiled at him sweetly. "Where he goes, I go."

The doctor shrugged. He and the nurse wheeled Ian's bed toward the door.

"You're bossy," Ian muttered as he was rolled past her and out into the hall.

She couldn't help the grin. "Yes, I am."

Deputy Chase Fredrick jumped to his feet and fell into step with Simone. "What's happening?"

"They need to run some tests." She addressed a passing nurse. "Can you please make sure that Mr. Delaney's family and the sheriff know he's being taken for scans?"

The nurse blinked at her and looked to Dr. Anders, who nodded and said, "That would be helpful, Janice." She hurried to the nurses' station.

A short ride in the elevator took them to the floor of the CT scan room.

Dr. Anders stopped Simone and Chase from following them inside. "You two will have to wait in there." He pointed to a glass-enclosed space.

Taking a post near the door, Simone crossed her arms and braced her feet apart as she watched the technicians transfer Ian onto the scanner table.

"He's going to be okay, right?" Chase asked.

Slanting the young deputy a glance, she answered, "I believe so. I'm sure the doc will tell us for sure. What do you know about Ian Delaney?"

"The Delaneys are an interesting family," Chase said. "A while back we had some trouble when his father created a treasure hunt that brought some very nasty people to our town. The treasure hunters burned down the sheriff's department building, and the Delaneys rebuilt it."

"I've heard the Delaneys are philanthropic. But what about Ian Delaney specifically? How well do you know him?"

"Not well, truth be told," Chase answered. "He has helped out the department on numerous occasions with his helicopter. He keeps to himself when he's in town. Not that he's reclusive or anything, but *aloof* is the only word that comes to mind."

"Not unusual for man of his affluence and prominence," Simone said.

"I guess. His younger brother's not like that at all,"

Chase said. "Nick has thrown himself into our community. He married one of our deputies. They recently adopted a child and are expecting one of their own now."

The door behind them was pushed open and Sheriff Alex Trevino stepped inside the glass-encased observation space. He was a tall man with wide shoulders and sandy-blond hair. Simone had met him briefly the last time she was in Bristle Township while guarding the adopted daughter of Nick Delaney.

"How is our patient?"

"Waiting to see, boss," Chase said.

Alex nodded. "I can take it from here, Chase. Check in with Daniel. He's holding down the fort. Then go home to your lovely wife."

Chase gave a mini salute and headed out the door.

Alex turned to Simone. "What have you learned so far?"

"Not much," she answered. "Did the forensics reveal anything useful?"

"Nothing beyond the sabotage," Alex replied. "Whoever tampered with the helicopter covered their tracks."

"Hopefully, Mr. Delaney will provide the needed info for your investigation."

Alex remained silent for a heartbeat then turned to stare her in the eyes. "Someone went to great lengths attempting to kill Ian."

"I won't let anything happen to Mr. Delaney," she assured him.

He gave a sharp nod.

The doctor stepped into the room. "We're done," he announced. "The nurse will take Mr. Delaney back to his room."

"How is he?" Alex asked.

"The radiologist and I will review the scan and give you an answer soon," Dr. Anders promised.

Alex and Simone filed out and followed the nurse wheeling Ian's bed back to his hospital room. Once Ian was hooked back up to the machines monitoring his heart rate and blood pressure, and an IV drip was rehydrating his body, the nurse left.

Ian turned to Alex. "I'm glad to see you, Sheriff. How did I get to Bristle Township?"

Alex frowned. "You don't remember?"

He didn't remember? Really? Simone moved closer, watching Ian for any sign of duplicity.

"No." Ian glanced at her and then back to Alex. "The last thing I recall is sitting at my desk."

"Where was that?" Simone asked.

Ian's gaze met hers. "At the company headquarters in Boston."

Surprise and disbelief mingled, raising Simone's tension. She exchanged a glance with Alex. "You have no recollection of why you were flying over the forest?"

"No. By 'forest,' do you mean the one here in Bristle County surrounding Bristle Township?" There was no mistaking the confusion in his tone.

"Yes," Alex said. "Apparently, you flew out of Boston on your jet three days ago. When you landed at the airstrip at the mountaintop resort, you took off in your helicopter. You didn't file a flight plan, which isn't unusual. However, a few hours later, the distress signal from your chopper was picked up by the airport's control tower. It took us several hours to find you and the wreckage on the backside of the mountain."

Ian stared at the ceiling. "Why don't I remember any of this?" He pinned Alex with his stare. "Was I alone?"

"There were witnesses on the ground who saw you get into the helicopter and take off. Alone," Alex said.

"You have no memory of any of this?" Simone couldn't keep the doubt out of her voice. Was he really suffering from amnesia or was he faking it?

"No, I don't." Ian's voice was resolute. "If I did, I would tell you."

Just because he said the words didn't make Simone believe him.

She'd dealt with numerous witnesses and CEOs claiming their innocence of any wrongdoing when their lives were at stake, only to find out the hard way they'd been lying. Not all, but some. Suspicion was part of her warning system and had kept her alive on more than one occasion. Better not to trust and expect everyone to be guilty of something than to be caught unaware and fail at her job.

She'd allowed that to happen once. Though Beth's death hadn't been during an assignment, Simone had let her guard down and her best friend had paid the price.

"Earlier, you asked me what kind of trouble I was in," Ian said, drawing her attention. "What did you mean?"

"Your crash was no accident," Simone told him.

"Someone put marbles in the gear box," Alex said.

"The big question is, Mr. Delaney…" Simone said. "Who wants you dead?"

Sharp pain splintered through Ian's head on a rhythmic cadence that would have brought him to his knees if he hadn't already been lying down. Simone's question reverberated through his brain and his body like shock waves bouncing off concrete.

Someone wanted him dead. His helicopter had been

sabotaged, and he had no memory of what he'd been doing in the air. Or why he'd left Boston. Distress was an unfamiliar sensation. One he didn't like.

"Mr. Delaney, can you walk us through what you do remember?"

The voice of his bodyguard drew his focus.

There was challenge in her gaze. Obviously, she didn't believe he'd lost his memory. Her beautiful dark eyes reminded him of polished onyx, deep and fathomless. He had the distinct impression she wasn't a fan. Not that he needed her to be, but if she were going to protect him, shouldn't she at least pretend some sympathy?

He took several deep breaths, calming his racing heart as he studied this very beautiful, intense woman.

Long dark hair pulled back in a serviceable clip at her nape showed off the slender column of her neck. The tone of her skin suggested she spent time in the sun, though there were no wrinkles or sun damage, so he imagined her glow was natural. It contrasted sharply with the white of her button-down shirt. Her black pantsuit hugged every curve and emphasized her long, lean legs. She wore the outfit well, like a shield.

A bodyguard. He knew enough about James Trent to know that he recruited from various law enforcement and military types. She was definitely ex-something or other. There was an air of authority and self-sufficiency about her that he'd seen on many men and women who worked in uniform.

Pushing through the throbbing in his mind, he thought back to the last day he could recall. "I remember that morning. Nothing unusual about it. I dressed, had coffee and went to the office. I sat down at my desk…" The ache behind his eyes increased. "But that's where my memory ends. I can't recall what I was doing at my desk."

A deep-seated panic fluttered in his chest. The last time he'd felt anything close to such unwanted awareness was when his mother had passed away.

What had happened to put his life in jeopardy? He tried to sit up. Alex and Simone both rushed forward to stop him.

"You need to rest and let your body heal," Alex admonished. "We don't know what's happening inside your head. The doctor will give us a diagnosis as soon as he reviews the scans from your tests."

Anger pushed the panic aside. Someone had robbed him of his memory and tried to kill him. He wanted to know who and why. He would not sit passively by while whoever had done this to him was on the loose. "I want out of here."

Simone patted his shoulder with enough force to propel him back against the pillows propping up his back. "What you need to do right now is let us do our jobs and protect you. When you're healthy enough to leave, we'll leave. Your family will be here any moment."

The familiar burn of frustration churned in his gut. His family had to be beside themselves with worry. Without him guiding the ship, they would be lost. His insides twisted with a different kind of anxiety. It was his job to keep his family from harm. Yet he couldn't even keep himself safe. His fingers curled at his sides. He hated this helpless feeling stealing over him.

The door opened and his father, a worried expression darkening his brown eyes, gripped his plaid blanket with one hand and motioned impatiently from his wheelchair for Nick to push him further inside the room with the other. His brother was dressed casually, as had become Nick's habit of late. Jeans and a long-sleeved pullover, no doubt picked out by his wife. Pretty in her understated way, Deputy Kaitlyn Lanz-Delaney, followed close behind them. Her blond hair loose, she also wore jeans and a lightweight sweater in a soft pink, making her appear anything but a deputy.

On Kaitlyn's hip was their adopted daughter, Rosie, a sweet, dark-haired child who had captured all of their hearts.

Simone and Alex moved away to allow his family closer access. Ian tried to answer the barrage of questions the trio asked as best he could. All the while, he could sense Simone watching from the corner. Her presence was both disconcerting and comforting.

Dr. Anders stepped into the room. After greetings were made, he announced, "No swelling on the brain, no discernible damage."

Ian breathed out a half measure of relief. "Except I've lost my memory leading up to the crash, so that's an issue."

Mild surprise flashed in the doctor's eyes. "Post-traumatic amnesia can occur after a head injury. Your memories may return on their own as you heal. We'll keep you another night for observation and do some more testing."

Ian's stomach sank. He didn't want to remain in the hospital, but as he looked at the beloved faces of his family, he realized it would be better if he stayed far away from them. He didn't want to put them in danger, too. "I'd like to rest now. I love you all." He purposely infused a note of dismissal in his tone.

"You heard the boy," Patrick said in his brittle voice.

He seemed to wheeze a bit as he breathed. "Time for us to go." He reached up to touch Ian's fisted hand, his fingers cool. "We're only a phone call away. We'll be back tomorrow to check on you."

Ian's heart squeezed at his father's frailty. His mother and father had had children late in life. Growing up with parents the age of the grandparents of his contemporaries had always made Ian feel a bit out of step with the rest of the world. But then again, he rarely fit in well, no matter the circumstance. He'd grown used to being the misfit.

Kaitlyn stepped forward and kissed his cheek. Her growing belly bumped against the side of the bed. She and Nick were expecting a baby next spring. Rosie snaked her arms around Ian's neck and he winced as she pressed a noisy kiss against his swollen lips. He couldn't begrudge her. He had never experienced the love of a child before Nick and Kaitlyn had bought Rosie home. He couldn't imagine anything happening to her because of him.

Kaitlyn set Rosie on Patrick's lap and wheeled them out of the room, leaving Nick behind. Clearly, his brother had words to say.

Instead of addressing Ian, Nick turned to Simone and Alex. "You have to find out who did this and why. This can't go unpunished."

Alex stepped forward. "You have my word. We are investigating to the best our ability."

"I know that, Alex, and I trust you." Nick turned to Simone. "I trust that you will protect my brother just as you protected my daughter."

"Of course," Simone replied. "You know I will."

Ten months ago, Nick had reached out to Trent Associates to protect Rosie and the staff at the estate, while

Nick and Kaitlyn uncovered the mysterious reason why Rosie's mother had perished in a car accident.

Nick turned back to Ian, his face grim—a look Ian wasn't used to seeing on his brother. Normally, Nick made light of most everything in life—his coping mechanism. "You are the rock of this family. We need you." Nick put his hand on Ian's shoulder. "Let Simone and Alex do their jobs and you do yours by healing. No heroics, you hear me?"

Ian tried to grin, but was sure his attempt looked grotesque given the way Nick winced. "Put yourself in my shoes. You would do whatever it took to find out the truth."

Nick sighed. "Yes, I would, and I'm going to. You can count on me. But you need to listen to your bodyguard. For the first time in your life, you are not the boss here. Don't let your ego get the better of you."

Another bubble of frustration jetted through Ian. With his father's frail health, Ian had taken on the role of head of the family, therefore he was the one they were all supposed to count on, not the other way around. He didn't need his brother lecturing him on how to conduct himself, either.

Once Nick left and it was just the sheriff and Simone in the room with him, Ian addressed Alex. "Keep me updated on any and everything you find out." He could see the man wanted to argue. "Alex, don't cut me out of the loop trying to protect me. The best way for you to protect me is to give me information."

Alex gave a beleaguered sigh. "Ian, this town owes you a lot. Not only did you rebuild the sheriff's department after it burned down, you've helped by using your helicopter during several search and rescues, including when Maya, Brady and I were being hunted on the mountain. I owe you a lot. I will tell you what you need to know when you need to know it." He then focused on Simone. "We are all trusting you to keep him safe, not only from the bad people who want him dead, but also from himself."

Ian barely refrained from snorting in protest. Like anyone could control him. He didn't need a babysitter. He needed answers.

"Roger that," Simone said, her gaze cutting to Ian's with purpose in the dark depths. She really was pretty and feisty. And there was something about her that made him want to know more, to dig deep into her mind and find out what made her tick. Not a usual occurrence for him. Must be the pain medications or the bump to his head.

Alex gave a sharp nod and left the room.

Ian stared at Simone, who stared back at him unflinching. He let out an aggravated breath. He doubted she'd let him past her stoic walls, even if he tried. "This is maddening."

"I would imagine so," she said crisply. "The best thing you can do for yourself is to heal and to let your brain remember what happened. And the only way you're going to do that is if you rest. I'm going to draw the blinds, shut the lights off and pray you'll uncover the secrets locked inside your mind with some sleep."

He'd pray so, as well.

Why did he take comfort in knowing she was a woman who prayed?

In the darkened room, he could barely make out her silhouette as she moved to the corner and sat in the chair. He doubted he'd be able to rest with her only a few feet away. She gave off such a dynamic energy that he felt buffered by it. But her words were true. If he could remember what happened, what had sent him out in his helicopter, it would save all of them a great deal of grief and send her on her way. And that would be the best thing for them all, because he had a feeling spending time with Simone wouldn't be easy. A thought he didn't want to examine.

He closed his eyes and sent up a prayer that God would bring the memories back. He willed his body to relax and cleared his mind, allowing sleep to claim him.

Hours later, Ian awoke with a start. Somebody hovered at the side of his bed. He blinked the sleep away to realize a male nurse was about to put a syringe into his IV line. Was he scheduled for some sort of medication the doctor neglected to mention?

The green glow from the monitors illuminated the menace in the man's face.

"Hey!" Ian grabbed for the hand with the syringe.

The door to his room's small bathroom burst open and light spilled out, silhouetting Simone in the doorway. "What are you doing?" Simone's voice cut through the tension of the room.

The nurse spun toward Simone then moved out of Ian's line of sight. There was a scuffle, a curse and then the door to the room banged open, allowing the light from the hall to spill inside, stinging Ian's eyes.

His heart hammered in his chest. He yanked the IV catheter from his hand, flinching at the sharp bite of pain.

Someone had just tried to kill him.

Again.

TWO

Simone tackled the man dressed in scrubs in the doorway of Ian's hospital room, the clatter of the syringe hitting the floor echoing in her ears. She landed on him with an *oof*. He twisted and bucked in an attempt to dislodge her. She used her elbow to deliver a blow to the side of his head. "Stop moving!"

Seated beside the door, a deputy she didn't recognize jumped to his feet and piled on. Together they managed to subdue the man.

The deputy, whose name tag read Rawlings, clapped handcuffs on the suspect, shoved him into the chair he'd just vacated and then looked at Simone. "What gives?"

Simone's heart pounded in her throat. "He had a syringe and was attempting to put something into Ian's IV. I'd made a point of meeting all the nurses scheduled to care for Ian, and he wasn't one of them. Plus, he's wearing Italian loafers. What nurse wears leather shoes on shift?"

She pushed to her feet to search for the syringe. She found the offending piece of medical equipment underneath Ian's bed.

"Tell me what's going on!" Ian demanded. He'd worked his way to a near sitting position.

"I don't know yet," she said. "Sit tight."

He huffed out an irritated breath. Simone empathized with him. It would be hard for someone like Ian, a man used to being in charge, to be sidelined while others fought for him. Too bad. He'd have to get used to it.

Grabbing a Kleenex from the counter, she picked up the syringe and hurried out the door.

"What's in this?" she demanded.

The fake nurse looked at her, his chin jutted in a mutinous way that told her he wasn't going to answer her questions.

Hospital staff gathered around. A dark-haired nurse, whom Simone had met earlier in the evening, stepped forward. "I need to check on my patient."

"Go ahead." Simone positioned herself so she could keep an eye on the brunette. "His hand is bleeding."

Deputy Rawlings held out an evidence bag.

She dropped the syringe into it. "Take that to the sheriff and have it analyzed. I don't think any was administered but, thankfully, Ian removed the IV."

Quick thinking on his part. She had to give him chops for having the mental awareness to know he needed to be rid of the IV in case any of the solution in the syringe had made it into the line.

"I'm not leaving," Deputy Rawlings said. "But I'll let the sheriff know. Our forensic tech will come get it." He moved a couple of steps away and spoke into the mic on his shoulder.

Simone turned her gaze back to the man sitting in the chair. Scruffy around the edges, with brown hair pulled back into a man bun, and a goatee. The pupils of his green eyes were dilated. Was he on something?

A man dressed in a hospital security uniform pushed through the nurses and doctors.

"We had a breach at the employee entrance," the young man said.

That only confirmed this as another attempt on Ian's life. Simone turned to the assailant. "Who sent you? What was in the syringe? Why are you doing this?"

The attacker stared at the floor before lifting his gaze. "Lawyer."

Deputy Rawlings walked back over. "The sheriff is on his way and so is our forensic tech."

"He lawyered up," she said.

Annoyance crossed the deputy's face. "Figures."

"Do you have him?" She gestured with her chin at the assailant.

"Yes," Deputy Rawlings replied. He put his hand on his holstered sidearm. "He's not going anywhere except jail."

"Let me know when Sheriff Trevino arrives," Simone said and stepped back inside Ian's room, shutting the door firmly.

She leaned her head against the cool wood surface. She'd almost failed to keep Ian safe. She hadn't heard the attacker walk in. But then again, the assassin hadn't wanted to be heard.

Still, she should have been more alert.

Her stomach knotted. She couldn't let a mistake like that happen again. To do so might cost Ian Delaney his life. And put another scar on her conscience.

The adrenaline spike of fear had ebbed away, leaving Ian exhausted. He watched Simone taking deep breaths and noisily exhaling. No doubt his bodyguard had felt the same jolt of panic he had. But she'd acted. She hadn't been stuck in a bed with monitors and a feeble body.

Gratitude for her quick reflexes filled him. "Are you okay?" Had she been hurt in the scuffle? He hated the thought of her injured. Another person for him to feel responsible for.

She pushed away from the door and strode purposely toward him. "That was close. I apologize. It won't happen again."

He frowned in confusion. "No apology necessary. It wasn't your fault. The man was dressed as a nurse. They come in and out of hospital rooms all the time. I've been with my father and my mother enough when they were hospitalized to know the drill."

She cocked her head. "I was sorry to read that your mother passed when you were a teen. Hodgkin's lymphoma, correct?"

"Yes." Old pain surfaced, making his throat tight. "She could have lived longer had she not refused to admit there was something wrong."

The sadness he always worked to keep at bay crept in. Not only had he and Nick lost their mother, their father had lost the love of his life. As a result, Patrick Delaney had devoted himself to his work, becoming a shell of his former self. A fate Ian never wanted to face. He'd rather never love and skip the pain of heartbreak than succumb to a broken heart.

Needing to redirect his thoughts, he said, "You have a file on me?"

A small smile played at the corners of her lush mouth. "Part of protection detail is to know as much as possible about the principle."

Meaning him. "Makes sense, but still, it seems invasive."

"I can understand that," she said. "But it's necessary."

He refrained from commenting that he didn't like that she knew more about him than he knew about her, which only served to pique his curiosity about her even more. "What did you learn from the fake nurse?"

"He lawyered up. We might not learn anything from him for a while, if ever."

The answers they needed were locked inside Ian's head. He wished he could remember. "I must know something that threatens these people."

"Agreed. Obviously, they know where you are. We're going to have to make different arrangements."

His thoughts went to the estate. It was a nearly impenetrable fortress. Yet his father, the staff, his brother and his new family were there. Ian would never put them in jeopardy.

Last year, when Nick and Kaitlyn had stayed at the estate to keep little Rosie safe, the house had come under attack on several occasions. Thankfully, it had never been breached, but Ian wouldn't take the risk.

And Ian certainly wouldn't ask his family to leave. What if whoever was after Ian went after his family while they were away from the security of the estate? "We have to figure this out. The only way to do that is for me to go back to Boston."

Simone remained silent for a moment, as if processing his comment. Then she slowly nodded. "I could keep you safe in Boston. We have safe houses there. Plus, there would be reinforcements. I'll talk with James to see what we can arrange."

It felt good to have a semiplan. Making one and executing it gave him a sense of purpose. He liked the feeling of accomplishment that came with a job well done. This would be no exception. "Good. And you'll help me retrace my steps. We'll start at my office."

She looked at him with an arched eyebrow. "You tell me I'm bossy?"

He liked the way her eyes danced with amusement. "It takes one to know one."

She gave a small laugh, the sound pleasing. Unaccountably, he had a feeling his earlier assessment of working with Simone Walker might be off. He might actually enjoy this as long as she realized he was in control.

Taking charge of the transfer of Ian to a safe house in Boston took a lot of coordination, not to mention cajoling Ian's family, who wanted him within the bosom of the family estate. But Simone understood Ian's vehement protest. He didn't want to put his family in danger. An admirable gesture.

The man certainly had persuasive powers and seemed to genuinely care about those around him. His concern for her after she'd taken down the attacker had surprised her. Most protectees expected their bodyguards to take whatever injuries befell them without comment.

Under heavily guarded escort, with the cooperation of the Bristle Township Sheriff's Department and the Colorado state police, they'd moved Ian from the hospital to a black Escalade. They'd then driven him to the Denver airport, where he and Simone took the Delaney private jet—with additional armed guards provided by Trent Associates—and flown to Boston's Logan International Airport. Even more guards had accompanied Simone and Ian to the safe house.

Finally, the constriction in Simone's chest eased and she could take a full breath.

As safe houses went, this one was top-notch. A well-appointed, luxury apartment on the top floor of a towering high-rise in the Back Bay neighborhood, not far from the Trent Associates office. The apartment would provide the kind of security she needed for Ian's protection.

The apartment had a three-sixty view of the Charles River, Boston and Cambridge skylines, which she barely glanced at as she secured all the windows and drew the blinds closed.

"Only someone with superhuman, spiderlike abilities would be able to climb up here," Ian said.

From his place on the posh leather couch, Ian tracked her with his eyes. She knew this because every time she glanced over, their gazes collided. The swelling around his face had lessened, but her awareness of him as an attractive man had only increased, much to her irritation.

"Would you please settle down?" he said. "You're making me nervous."

He was right, of course. No one could get to them on the eighteenth floor, but that didn't mean she shouldn't take precautions. Just as she would take precautions to ensure she stayed emotionally safe from the too handsome man.

She turned and gripped the back of the dining room chair in front of her, forcing her expression to remain impassive. "We don't know that we weren't followed here. We can take all the safeguards we want, but if somebody's motivated enough, they'll always find a way."

"Well, that's reassuring."

She winced at his dry comment and the underlining

note of alarm. Keeping him safe also meant keeping him calm. "I just want you to be very aware of the stakes."

"I am aware, thank you." There was no mistaking the irritation in his tone. She didn't blame him for being upset. This was a stressful situation and she had to admit that, so far, he was holding up well.

He breathed in as if to rein his ire. "I really appreciate how you navigated my family. They can be a lot sometimes."

She smiled at the assessment. "Trust me, I know something about families who can be a handful." With two older brothers and protective parents to contend with, she had experience in the delicate balance of making sure those she loved were heard, even if she didn't always take their advice.

He patted the seat cushion next to him. "Come sit here and tell me about you. I know next to nothing about the woman I'm entrusting my life to."

A fair enough request. She moved across the room, but instead of sitting next to him on the couch, which screamed of an intimacy she wasn't about to share with the good-looking billionaire client, she took one of the side chairs. Safer that way.

Kicking off her flats, she tucked her feet underneath her. She would be glad when she could change out of these clothes and into something less constricting. But she couldn't ever relax. Not fully. The incident in the hospital had proved that.

She glanced at the alarm panel near the front door. Watching the little green blinking light reassured her for the hundredth time that the apartment security system was armed and ready.

When she turned her focus back to Ian, the expectation in his warm brown eyes had her contemplating just how much to reveal of herself. For some reason, she wanted to open up to this man, something she rarely did. But getting close to a principle was *not* something she could allow. It wouldn't be professional or smart. "My family immigrated to the US from Trinidad and Tobago to Detroit in the nineties. I was three years old."

Ian nodded. "My father brought our family from Ireland to the US when I was just a little over four and Nick was a baby."

She'd read that in his dossier. Interesting that they both had the common bond of not being native to the country they each lived in now.

"My mother went into law enforcement," she continued. "She worked her way up to chief of detectives for the Detroit PD. She recently retired, but she was a firecracker investigator."

"And you followed in her footsteps."

Her lips curved in a rueful smile. "Yes, I did. Police academy and patrol then homicide."

"Now bodyguard." His eyes burned with curiosity. "Why the change?"

Not prepared to answer at this time, if ever, she pushed up from the chair. He didn't need to know how she had failed to protect her best friend or the lengths she'd been willing to go to extract vengeance. Old grief and sorrow rubbed at the still-raw wound. "It's late. We both need rest. Tomorrow we'll go to your office and find out what you were doing the day you left Boston."

She helped him to his feet and to one of the en suite rooms. The bags he'd had brought from his home in Colorado lay on the floor. She hesitated at the door. "Do you need help?"

"I'll be fine," Ian said. "You've been more than enough help today. I can take care of myself."

She couldn't ignore his flinch as he stepped away from her. The man had been in a helicopter crash, after all. Quickly, she reclaimed his side, slipping her arm around his waist and guiding him to the bed where he gingerly sat on the edge.

He waved her off. "I've got this."

Moving away from him, she pointed to a small device on the bedside table. "You push that button and it rings throughout the whole apartment. You need anything, don't hesitate."

"You've thought of everything."

"Not me," she said. "James. My boss. He's been at this for a long time."

"I'll have to remember to thank him."

She nodded and dipped out the door.

In her own en suite room, she quickly changed into stretch pants and a T-shirt, thankful that her boss had had her to-go bag brought to the safe house. Then checked in with James, going over the arrangements for taking Ian to his company office in the morning.

After one more pass around the apartment, double-checking that all the windows were closed and locked, and the security alarm was armed, she couldn't keep the fatigue at bay any longer. Ian was as secure as she could make him for the time being. Tomorrow would be another day to worry about his welfare.

She would be no good to Ian if she didn't get some rest. She'd been up and going for the past thirty-two hours. Ever since she'd received the call to head to Colorado.

Opting to sleep on the couch in the living room, just

in case, she grabbed the pillow from her bed and a blanket. She kept her firearm close. Protecting Ian was her job and she would not fail.

The next morning, Ian awkwardly dressed in slacks and a dress shirt. He wanted to shave, but with his swollen eye and the aches and pains everywhere else, he decided to forgo the razor. Everyone was just going to have to live with the stubble for now.

The smell of bacon and eggs drew him slowly out of his room and into the kitchen. Simone wore a white bib apron over a burgundy-colored, two-piece pant suit and a light pink button-down shirt. Her dark hair was twisted into a knot at the back of her head. He really wanted to see her hair down and loose. Would the strands be silky soft or textured against his skin?

She met his gaze and he could feel a flush of embarrassment creep up his neck. What on earth was he doing thinking about touching her hair? She was his bodyguard, not a potential romantic interest. Not that he dated much. Keeping his heart under wraps was as important to him as the company making a wide profit margin every year.

Simone set down the spatula in her hand and rushed around the kitchen island to wrap an arm around his waist to help him to the dining room table. He should protest. He was capable of making it on his own, but he couldn't deny how nice it felt to lean on her, to smell the citrusy scent of her shampoo. It had been too long since he'd had any female company.

"Did you get some rest?" she asked.

"I slept like the dead." He winced. "Wrong choice of words."

"Indeed."

He settled in his seat at the table and she went back to the kitchen. A few seconds later, she brought him a plate with several slices of bacon and perfectly cooked fluffy eggs. She set a fork and a glass of orange juice down in front of him, as well.

"Eat up," she said. "You'll need your strength."

"Aren't you going to join me?"

"Yes, I am." She brought her own plate of food to the table and sat across from him.

They ate in companionable silence. It was nice not to have the urge to fill the space between them with talk. And he liked the way she ate with gusto. He appreciated women who weren't afraid to have an appetite. Though, to be fair, he figured she probably worked out to keep her slim physique.

When the breakfast dishes were cleaned and put away, he watched Simone tuck her firearm into a shoulder holster underneath her suit jacket.

A stark reminder of the danger lurking outside the safety of the apartment.

He almost asked her for a weapon but decided he was in no condition to handle a gun. Though his right eye wasn't as swollen this morning, his vision wasn't 100 percent.

At the back exit of the apartment building, two armed men waited. Once Simone hustled Ian into the back of the black SUV and then settled in beside him, the two men got in the front.

Simone made the introductions. "Johnny Cruz and Milo Yang, Ian Delaney."

The men nodded a greeting.

"Where to?" Johnny, a burly man with muscles that

were unmistakable beneath his dark suit, fired up the engine.

His partner, Milo, wasn't nearly as bulky, but Ian sensed the man was probably equally deadly. He'd moved with a lethal grace that spoke of the man's agility. Ian wouldn't want to tangle with either of the men.

Ian gave Johnny the address to the Delaney Holdings office building. They drove through light traffic and arrived without incident, for which Ian was grateful. He sent up a quick praise to God for the small favor. His bodyguards hustled him inside the lobby.

The building security guard, Tim rushed forward. The older gentleman, wearing a green sport coat with the company's logo on the breast pocket, had a concerned expression on his lined face. "Mr. Delaney! We heard about your accident. You look awful."

Johnny and Milo blocked Tim.

"It's okay, I know Tim." Ian chuckled as he stepped around the two men. "I appreciate the feedback."

Tim flushed red. "Sorry, sir. It's just, we didn't expect you back anytime soon."

"I'm sure you didn't." Ian gestured to his entourage. "We're going up."

Tim hurried to the bank of elevators. Using his key card, he let them into the private elevator that would take them to the floors occupied by Delaney Holdings.

On the fourteenth floor, Ian led them to his corner office, all the while nodding and murmuring greetings to the staff who expressed surprise at seeing him and wished him well.

His assistant, Phyllis Bixby, jumped when she saw him, her blue eyes rounding behind her colorfully framed glasses. In her midfifties, Phyllis had been with Delaney

Holdings for the past twenty years. She wore her salted brunette hair short, the ends curling around her face and giving her a pixie sort of look. But, as always, she was dressed impeccably in a powder-blue skirt, matching heels and a cream-colored blouse. "Ian, what happened? We heard you were in a helicopter crash and that you were in the hospital. Why are you here? You should be home recovering."

"I need something from my office, Phyllis," he said.

She tsked her disapproval.

Ian was used to her mothering, so he assured her, "We'll only be here for a short time."

He opened the door to his office and strode inside, stopping abruptly at the sight that met him. The office had been ransacked. Papers strewn all over the floor. The bookshelves upended. His wall safe raided.

A deep sense of violation hit Ian in the chest. Had his attackers found what they were looking for? And if so, what had been worth trying to kill him?

THREE

Behind Ian and the bodyguards, Phyllis gasped. "Oh, no! When did this happened? I haven't been in here since you left last Tuesday. Nobody's been in here as far as I know."

Ian seethed. Obviously, someone had infiltrated their secure building. Unless…an employee? He couldn't fathom that one of the men or women in his employ would try to kill him, let alone tear apart his office. For what reason?

Simone walked past him to survey the damage then turned to look at Ian and his assistant. "I need you both to assess what's missing—but don't touch anything."

Easier said than done. Ian walked farther into the room, careful not to step on papers or books. Glass from broken picture frames littered the gray carpet and glinted in the morning sun streaming through the floor-to-ceiling windows. His desk drawers had been pulled open and left agape, the contents spilled on the floor. His desktop computer had been smashed, as if in a fit of rage.

Simone addressed Milo. "Inform James that there's been a breach in the Delaney offices. We need a full dossier on every person who has access to this floor, including the security guards." Milo nodded and walked out.

Ian faced her. "Tim didn't have anything to do with this. I've known the man my whole adult life."

Simone ignored his comment and talked to Johnny. "Call the local police and ask for a forensic unit. Nobody gets in here until the police arrive." He nodded and stepped out, shutting the door behind them.

Phyllis moved to the bookcase and reached to right a framed photograph.

"Don't touch!" Simone fairly barked. "Take a visual perusal and see if there's anything obvious gone."

Ian's heart sank. He couldn't think of anything he kept in this office that was worth stealing, letting alone attempting to do him in. He moved to the safe, which was now empty. He mentally ran through the contents.

Simone joined him. "What did you keep in there?"

"My US, Ireland and UK passports, some petty cash and a deposit box key."

"What do you keep in your safe-deposit box?"

"Nothing worth killing over," Ian replied. He thought about the last time he'd accessed his box, at least a year ago. "I have copies of the family wills. Some of my mother's jewelry. A few mementos that wouldn't mean anything to anyone but me."

"Call the bank. See if anyone has tried to access your box. If not, tell them your key has been stolen and to alert the authorities if anyone tries," Simone instructed.

He chaffed at being told what to do but acknowledged the logic of making the call. He took his cell phone from his pocket and dialed his bank.

"Phyllis," Simone said. "What's missing?"

The older woman shook her head. "Nothing of import that I can tell."

Ian hung up the call with the bank. Anger and frustration surged through him. "Someone posing as me came in two days ago and cleaned out the safe-deposit box."

"We'll ask the local police to pull the bank's video to see if they can identify the suspect," Simone said.

Pushing aside the disturbing thought that someone had his property, Ian focused on Phyllis. "What was I working on when I was here last?"

She thought for a moment before her face lit up. "You were going over the company's P and L reports. Then you buzzed and asked me to bring you the financials for the Dresden Group."

Dresden Group. He turned the name over in his head, but nothing clicked. He glanced down at the file folders and scattered pages on the floor. He had no recollection of making the request, let alone reviewing profit and loss reports. Heeding Simone's warning not to touch anything, Ian said, "Can you pull those files for me again, please?"

Phyllis's head bobbed. "Of course. I can do that." She opened the door, nearly ramming into Johnny. She sidestepped him and went to her desk. The bodyguard's eyebrows rose in question.

"We're good here," Simone said.

He nodded and shut the door again.

"What is this Dresden Group?" Simone asked.

Ian pinched the bridge of his nose. His head throbbed, pain radiating across his forehead and wrapping around his skull. "I have no idea. The name sounds familiar, but I can't recall why."

"It may come to you in time. Obviously, something

you were looking at sent you running back to Bristle Township."

"You're probably right. Once we see that report, we'll have a better understanding of what's going on." At least, he prayed so.

A few moments later, Phyllis walked in, wringing her hands. Concern darkened her blue eyes.

Dread knotted Ian's gut. "Phyllis, what is it?"

"Ian, I hate to say this, but the Dresden Group files are all gone."

"What do you mean gone?" That made no sense. "How can they be 'all gone'?"

She grimaced. "I don't know. They're not on our servers at all. I had IT double-check when I couldn't bring them up on my computer. There's no evidence of anything in our company records with the name Dresden Group."

Ian's fists clenched. There could only be one explanation. They'd been hacked. "I want to talk to the IT guy." He strode toward the door.

Simone blocked his path. "Where do you think you're going?"

"To the server room."

For a moment, he thought she would attempt to prevent him from leaving the office, but then she moved aside.

"Johnny, let me know when the police arrive," Simone said. "Milo and I will accompany Ian."

Ian led the way to the company's IT department. The men and women inside the cubicled space were frantically scrambling, no doubt trying to figure out when and how the breach in security had occurred.

The manager of the department hurried forward.

Kevin Strand wore round glasses that made him appear a bit owlish. His balding head glistened with a sheen of sweat. "Mr. Delaney, we are running every diagnostic possible. There's no sign of a breach in our system. And no sign whatsoever of this Dresden Group you were asking about. Whoever did this was good. Like, scary good. I've never seen such a clean wipe before."

Ian dragged a hand over his still sore and puffy jaw. Anxiety crept into his shoulders, making the muscles tense. "Could this be an inside job?"

Kevin's mouth opened then snapped shut. His eyes swung to his team. When he met Ian's gaze, he looked nauseous. "I'd hate to think so. But I will personally audit each station."

Ian had no choice but to trust that Kevin wasn't the one who'd wiped the servers of the Dresden Group files. "Let me know if you find anything. Can you also check the building security videos for anything suspicious?"

"We need to check the files on the floor in your office. Maybe the hard copy versions of the files are there. Or at least a stray page or something to give a clue what is in the files," Simone said.

He nodded, hoping her words were true, but he had a sinking feeling that the files were gone. And, with them, any hope of discovering the reason someone wanted him dead.

By the time they returned to his office, the police were there. The crime scene unit were in the process of dusting everything for fingerprints and combing through the space looking for trace evidence as to who might've broken in.

After taking Ian and Simone's statements, the officers began the arduous task of interviewing each employee as well as obtaining copies of the building's security tapes from Kevin in IT.

Several hours later, after being given the all-clear, Ian entered his office again. He gathered all the strewed papers and read each one carefully but found nothing related to the Dresden Group.

Simone held up a square sticky note she found underneath his desk. "Any idea what this is?"

He studied the numbers and letters written at a diagonal. "No. But that's my writing. It could be a bank account number. Or a security code. Or password."

Simone tucked it into the pocket of her jacket.

Irritation and anxiousness warred within Ian. What happened to those files? They clearly had existed at one time. There was no reason to doubt Phyllis's memory for one second. And he paid the best of the best to keep his company from being hackable. He buzzed Phyllis. "Can you ask Kathleen O'Connell to come in, please?"

Simone quirked an eyebrow.

"The chief financial officer. She'll have to know something about the Dresden Group."

A few moments later, a knock on the door grabbed their attention.

"Come in," Ian called out.

Johnny opened the door. "Kathleen O'Connell is here to see you."

"Send her in," Simone instructed.

Ian slanted her a glance and refrained from commenting that this was his office, so he should be the one granting access. But he let it go.

Kathleen walked in, her bright auburn hair cascading down her back and held up at her temples with clips. Her bright green eyes were wide with worry as she rushed to

Ian's side and gripped his arm, her slender fingers digging into his flesh. Though she was over ten years his senior, she'd made it known on more than one occasion she'd be open to a relationship.

"Are you okay?" Her gaze went to Simone and then back to Ian. "We heard about the crash. Your father told us you were pretty banged up. I couldn't believe it when they said you were here in the office."

While he appreciated her concern, Ian extracted himself from her grasp. "I'm fine, as you can see."

Kathleen's lips pressed together in a tight smile and she turned her attention to Simone. "Hello." She held out her hand. "I'm Kathleen. And you are?"

Simone shook Kathleen's hand. "Simone."

"And how do you and Ian know each other?" the CFO asked her.

Ian frowned at the intrusive question. "We're friends."

Simone gave him a thoughtful look then said to Kathleen with a saucy smile, "Close friends."

Ian swallowed his surprise at Simone's implication that they had a romantic relationship. Did she not want anyone to know the true purpose of her presence? Deciding he'd delve into that mystery later, he asked Kathleen, "Tell me what you know about the Dresden Group."

Kathleen's eyebrows drew together. "Dresden Group? I don't know anything, really. It's a subsidiary that was put in place before my time here. In fact, I don't think there's been any activity in that group in over a decade or two."

"You wouldn't happen to have the files in your office, would you?"

She blinked and tucked in her chin. "Why would I

have those files on hand? I'm sure Phyllis can pull them off the servers for you."

Ian exhaled a frustrated breath.

"Actually, she can't," Simone said. "Your servers have been hacked. Anything relating to the Dresden Group has been erased."

Kathleen gasped. "That's not possible. How can we have missing files?"

"We'll be looking into the breach of security," Ian assured her.

Eyes wide, Kathleen's gaze bounced between Ian and Simone and then back to Ian. "You two?"

Simone waved a hand. "Of course not us." Her tone held a note of amusement that even to Ian's ears sounded real. "The police."

"Ah." Kathleen gave a slow nod.

"Haven't the police talked to you?" Simone asked. "They've been interviewing everyone this morning."

"I've been out of the office until now." Kathleen brushed her hands on her skirt. "I'm going to need to do a full financial audit of the whole company." She turned on her heels, rushed toward the door and then stopped to look back. "Was there anything else you needed, Ian?"

"No, Kathleen, there's not. Thank you."

Muttering to herself, she left.

As soon as the door shut behind Kathleen, Ian said, "'Close friends'? Now she thinks you're my girlfriend."

Simone shrugged. "Best not to advertise I'm your bodyguard."

He plopped down in his leather chair and immediately regretted the motion as pain reverberated up his spine, sending a fresh throbbing ache through to his brain. He rubbed his forehead. If only he could rub away the pain and bring back his memories.

Simone moved to his side, her light touch on his shoulder drawing his gaze. He liked the way the natural light from the windows softened her expression. "Could there be a chance you took the files home to your apartment? I would assume you had gone back there before you left Boston. To pack a bag or change clothes before heading out?"

He hadn't thought of that. "Maybe. It's worth a try."

With effort, he pushed to his feet. His body protested the exertion. But it could be worse. He could be dead.

"We should go back to the safe house and let you rest before we tackle your apartment." Simone peered at him, worry obvious in her dark eyes and lowered brows. Genuine anxiety? Or manufactured as part of her job?

"No." He steadied himself by bracing his feet apart. He didn't want her seeing him as someone weak she had to coddle. "I need to retrace my steps on that day. If I did leave here and go back to my place, then there might be something in the apartment that could tell us what is going on. I need to see this through and find out who's behind the attempts on my life and why." He strode across the room for the door. "It's the only way to keep my family safe and protect my company."

Simone matched him step for step, arriving at the door at the same time. She stayed his grip on the doorknob with her hand on his arm. Unlike when Kathleen had touched him, Simone's fingers created warm spots that seeped through his shirt into his skin. Decidedly pleasant.

"I agree, Ian. But my job is to protect you, and I can't let you collapse from exhaustion. You're still recovering from your injuries." Her firm tone couldn't mask the distress in her voice. Apparently, her concern was real.

He covered her fingers with his, enjoying the softness of her strong, capable hand. He respected her compassion when she could easily not care one way or the other. "After my apartment, we can go to the safe house and I'll sleep the rest of the day. I promise."

"I'll hold you to that promise." She slipped her hand from beneath his, leaving him feeling bereft of her touch, and opened the door.

"I have no doubt." Instinctively, he knew she was a woman of her word.

Back in the lobby of the building, he asked Tim to look at the logbooks to see who had come and gone from the building that was not an employee. All guests had to log in.

"There hasn't been anyone who didn't belong in the building for the past week," Tim stated.

"What about the maintenance people?" Simone asked.

Tim nodded. "The cleaning crew comes every night. But they're all bonded, and we've used the same service in the building for years."

Simone turned to Milo. "We need—"

Milo held up a hand. "Way ahead of you. The office is doing a workup on everyone who has access to the building, not just Delaney Holdings."

Simone smile. "Thank you. I appreciate it."

Milo and Johnny walked out the lobby doors first. Johnny headed for the driver's side of an SUV at the curb, while Milo opened the back door.

Simone held Ian back a second. "Hold up."

Unease slithered down his spine. "What is it?"

She put her hand on her weapon beneath her jacket. "A feeling. Something's not right."

Ian reached to pull her farther away from the entrance just as the crack of a rifle echoed through the air. The glass door in front of Ian burst into a million pieces. The swirl of air as the bullet zinged close to his head jolted him into action. He instinctively turned away from the spray of glass and grabbed for Simone, intending to pull her out of the line of fire.

Her hands wrapped around his biceps and she launched him to the ground, her body draping his. He struggled against her, wanting to reverse their positions so that he could shield her. He wasn't going to let her take a bullet for him. More bullets hit the entryway. Close. A shudder of fear racked him.

Milo rushed back into the building, covering Simone and Ian. Another shot took out the rear window of the SUV.

Johnny dove through the open passenger-side door and pinned his back to the front wheel. "Shots are coming from the park."

"Eyes on?" Simone called back.

"No. I missed the muzzle flash."

"Same," Milo said.

They were pinned down.

An assassin wanted Ian dead at any cost, and he feared his bodyguards were going to be the ones to pay the ultimate price. No way could he allow that.

"Stop squirming!" Simone barked at Ian when he leveraged himself up and tried to move from beneath the protective shield she and Milo provided. "You're going to get shot."

"So will you!"

Annoyance rushed through her veins. She didn't need him trying to play the hero. "Stay down." She turned to see Tim peeking around the guard station in the middle of the lobby. She called to him. "Call 9-1-1!"

The man nodded and ducked back as more bullets pelted the building.

She had to get Ian to safety. "Is there a rear entrance to this building?"

"Yes." Ian lifted his head and met her gaze. "Through the mail room."

Tapping Milo, she said, "I'm taking him out the back."

Milo gave her the thumbs-up sign. "We'll come around and pick you up."

"On three." To Ian, she said, "When I say go, we're running in a low crouch for the mail room. You lead the way."

"Got it."

"One. Two. Three!" She rolled aside so Ian could get his feet under him. Milo ran for the SUV. She and Ian raced in a crouch away from the main entrance. More bullets hit the marble flooring, spitting bits and pieces of the stone at their backs.

Ian slammed into a door to open it. His hand grabbed her arm and pulled her into a large room filled with mailboxes for the tenants of the building.

"This way." Ian pushed through another door to the building's garbage and recycling center. An exit sign above the door at the end of the space beckoned.

"Wait!" Simone shouted. The need for caution tripped down her spine. "Let me go first."

The people attempting to kill Ian could have another shooter covering the exit. They could be walking into a trap. She had to be ready to give her life. A small price to pay to keep Ian safe. She couldn't bear someone else losing their life because of her.

FOUR

His heart hammering against his rib cage, Ian pressed his back against the wall of the building's garbage and recycling room. The rancid odor of trash made his eyes water, but he was thankful to be alive. A sniper had nearly taken him and his protection detail out. He sent up a quick prayer of gratitude that no one had been hurt. Yet.

Next to him, Simone popped open the metal door leading to the alley behind the building and waited a second before she toed the opening wider. She remained motionless with her weapon in her hands.

Tension tightened Ian's gut. Was another shooter out there waiting to pick them off?

Questions swirled through his brain. Who was trying to kill him? Why? What connection was there to the Dresden Group? What was the Dresden Group? Who'd hacked their servers and removed all traces of this mysterious arm of Delaney Holdings?

He needed to talk to his father to find out what the elder Delany knew about the Dresden Group.

In his pocket, his phone buzzed like an annoying gnat. He quickly grabbed it and glanced at the device. At Simone's sharp look, he said, "My brother."

He flipped off the ringer and slipped the phone back into his pocket. There wasn't anything Nick could do from Colorado. The police had already been called by Tim, the security guard. Ian would check in with Nick later. If there was a later…

The sound of tires screeching on pavement filled the room. The shadow of the team's SUV darkened the exit.

"On three," Simone told Ian. With one hand, she tugged Ian out the door and practically shoved him into the vehicle's back seat. "Get down."

He hunched as the vehicle lurched into motion, keeping his head low within the SUV, as best as his six-foot-four frame would allow. Air from the shot-out back window churned through the interior, hot and humid, as Johnny drove at a breakneck speed down the back alley and out onto the main thoroughfare.

Milo turned in his seat. "James will meet us at the safe house."

"Good," Simone replied.

"Were we followed from the apartment to my office?" Ian had to shout over the noise of traffic and wind.

"Doubtful," Simone replied, leaning closer to his ear, a tendril of her silky hair brushing against his cheek like a caress. "More like someone at your office arranged for the hit."

All thoughts of silky hair fled. Her grim pronouncement jabbed him in the gut. Someone within his organization wanted him dead. He mentally ticked off the list of names under his employ, but not one rang alarm bells. The idea that someone he trusted had gone to such lengths to get rid of him created a distressing burn in his chest. Each person who worked for Delaney Holdings went through extensive vetting and background checks.

But that didn't mean he hadn't angered someone enough to commit violence.

Yet, for the life of him, he couldn't come up with a suspect or a motive. He always tried to be a fair and reasonable person. If someone had grievances against him or his business practices, there were certainly more civilized ways to resolve them.

They arrived at the safe house, and Simone hustled Ian inside. Johnny and Milo returned to Delaney Holdings to talk with the authorities.

Simone immediately set the alarm. "Take a seat on the couch."

He narrowed his gaze at her and remained rooted in place. "Shouldn't we talk to the police?"

"We will," she said. "When it's safe. Johnny and Milo are headed back to the crime scene. They will deal with the local law enforcement."

Accepting her words, Ian moved to the leather couch, noting the pillow and blanket stacked at one end. He hadn't realized she'd slept in the living room the night before. Her dedication to his protection was admirable and made him feel…a strange mix of gratitude and irritation. He didn't like having to rely on someone else. For anything.

But her job was to keep him safe.

He dropped his head into his hands as the adrenaline from the day ebbed away. Though he'd served in the air force, he'd never seen battle. Training exercises in the sky were as close to any real danger he'd experienced, until now.

He squared his shoulders and lifted his head to find Simone watching him, her gaze intent and assessing, exactly as she'd been when he'd first awoken in the hospital.

Under her scrutiny, his defenses rose. Why did he have the distinct feeling she didn't think much of him?

Needing to take control of the present situation, he stood. "I want to talk to my father. He will have information on this Dresden Group that can't be hacked."

She cocked an eyebrow. "Brilliant idea. And don't forget that Nick called."

Disconcerted because he had forgotten, he nodded. "Right."

He rang his father's private line. The call went to voice mail. It was unlike his father to not pick up. A bubble of apprehension tickled his throat.

Ian hit the call-back button for Nick's cell. His brother answered the first ring. "We're on our way to the hospital."

Knees buckling, Ian sank onto the couch. Had the person behind the attacks gone after his family, too? Ian's stomach dropped as his hand tightened around the phone. Had Nick's Rosie or Kaitlyn been hurt? Fear crowded his mind. "What's happening?"

"Dad's having trouble breathing," Nick said. "We're in the ambulance. As soon as I know more, I'll call you."

Sharp anguish stabbed at Ian. His father's health had been failing for a while now. Ian should be at his side. If his father passed... "I'll be there as soon as I can."

"Are you sure that's wise?" Nick asked.

"Family first, always," Ian said. "Keep me updated the second you hear anything."

Ian clicked off and strode toward the bedroom to collect his things.

Simone stepped into his path. "Excuse me. You'll be where?"

"My father is headed to the hospital. I have to go to him."

Simone shook her head. "Not acceptable. You have a target on your back."

"I'm aware of the risk," he said. "But my father needs me. I'm going. You can either do your job and protect me on the way, or I can ask James to assign me a new bodyguard."

Sparks flashed in her dark eyes. "If that is what you want."

He reined in his own anger. She was right to protest, and he shouldn't give her grief considering she'd saved his life twice already. But he wouldn't be able to live with himself if his father passed away while he was hiding in this apartment too afraid to be at his father's side. Ian took a breath and slowly exhaled. "What I want is to get back to Bristle Township, and I'd like you to accompany me."

For a long moment, she stared at him. No doubt she wanted to throttle him for not cooperating. He stood his ground. His family was his priority, always.

A determined gleam entered her eyes. "I'll talk to James about transportation. He should be here any minute now, so you'll have to wait until we can figure things out." She turned on her heel and walked into the kitchen.

Did that mean she would stay on as his bodyguard? He leaned against the island. "Thank you."

She reached in the refrigerator for two bottles of water and tossed one at him. "It's your neck on the line."

Hers, too, if she stayed on as his protector. Guilt pricked him. But it couldn't be helped. He needed someone watching his back, and he trusted her to be that person. Though he had no explanation for why. They'd only just met. But there was something compelling about the no-nonsense woman that intrigued him. She was beautiful, yes, but there was more than the outward package to Simone. And it had been a long time since he'd wanted to delve deeper into knowing another person.

He took a long swig of water, letting the liquid cool his thoughts. He needed to maintain his barriers. Getting to know Simone on a personal level would only muddle matters. He didn't want to add any more complications to his life.

A knock sounded at the apartment's front door.

"That will be James," Simone said. "But just in case, keep out of sight." With her hand on her weapon, she headed to the entryway.

Ian followed her and moved to the side of the door, close enough that he could grab her if things went south. Simone frowned at him then peered through the peephole. Visibly relaxing, she opened the door and stepped back to allow James Trent to enter.

Average in height, with a wiry frame, James exuded a frenetic vigor as he strode forward, pausing to sweep the room with his eyes. He spun to face Ian. "It's been a long time." He stuck out his hand.

Ian stepped closer and accepted the handshake. "Yes, it has, James. I do appreciate your help. I've been impressed with your team."

"They are impressive." Pride infused James's tone.

Impatience getting the better of him, Ian stated, "I need to get back to Bristle Township, ASAP."

James stared at him through a narrowed gaze. "You're safer here."

Simone quickly spoke up. "His father is on the way to the hospital."

Understanding widened James's eyes. "I see."

"I need to be with my family," Ian said. "Can you make arrangements?"

"Hmm. Yes. We would follow the same procedure we did bringing you out," James replied. "However, the more you're exposed, the more risk there is that the people who want you dead will succeed."

"I'm aware," Ian said, slanting a quick look at Simone. She raised an eyebrow, as if daring him to refute her boss's warning. "It's a risk I'm willing to take. I have to be with my family."

James's assessing once-over raked Ian in a way that few dared. But Ian kept his stance steady. He would not be dissuaded.

Abruptly, James turned to Simone. "And are *you* willing?"

Ian focused on her, praying she'd say yes. He trusted her in ways he couldn't explain. That didn't make sense, but none of this made any sense. If only his memory would return, he could put an end to this whole ordeal.

Simone gave a sharp nod. "He's my assignment. I won't let you down."

An unexpected wave of relief that she'd be the one protecting him hit Ian even as her words registered. She talked as if he wasn't standing right there. And why did hearing her call him "my assignment" cause a strange sort of annoyance to scratch at the middle of his chest?

James's gaze softened. "You never do, Simone." He clapped his hands. "All right then. We have work to do to get you home to your family, Ian. We will need reinforcements. I just talked to Johnny before I came up. He said the local authorities didn't find anything to indicate the identity of the shooter. Whoever the sniper was did a clean job."

"Not too clean," Simone said. "They missed."

Barely. Ian's stomach roiled. It had been close enough that he'd swear under oath in a court of law he'd felt a bullet whiz past his ear and embed itself in the building's wall. Giving credit where credit was due, he said, "I'm only alive because of the quick thinking of Simone and your other operatives."

James gave a pleased nod. "I hire only the best. But even the best sometimes fail."

Ian noted that Simone's gaze dropped briefly to the floor before she straightened her spine and squared her shoulders. "Not always. And not this time."

What did she mean? Had she failed in the past? Curiosity to know more about this enigmatic woman burned in Ian's gut. But appeasing his desire to delve into her life wasn't a good idea. He didn't want to get attached to his bodyguard.

Better to return his attention to the matter at hand. Someone had ransacked his office, wiped his servers clean of all traces of the Dresden Group and then tried to kill him. Could the answers be at his place? "We need to search my apartment for the files."

Simone quickly brought James up to speed on where they were with the Dresden Group.

"You believe your father might have pertinent information?" James asked.

"I do." His heart squeezed tight. "Assuming I'm able to talk to him." A sense of urgency zipped along his limbs. "I have to get back there. My family needs me."

"I'll have Milo and Johnny stop by your apartment. Do you have a key?"

Ian dug the access card out of his pocket and handed it to James.

"Give me a half hour. As soon as the state troopers are mobilized and the jet is fueled, we'll get you back to Colorado."

Ian appreciated James's efficiency. His phone trilled in his pocket. His brother. Dread crept into his lungs, trapping his breath. He hit the answer button. "Nick."

"They took Dad in for tests. It doesn't look good, Ian. How soon can you get here?"

Anguish flooded his veins. "I'm working on it now with James and Simone."

"Kaitlyn and I will pray for your safe return. I've got to go." His brother clicked off.

Ian gripped the phone. A gentle hand covered his fist. He met Simone's sympathetic eyes.

"I'm sorry this is happening right now," she said, her voice low, soothing. "We're going to do everything we can to make sure you get there in one piece. We can only pray it will be in time."

Touched by her words, he nodded and lifted up a prayer for safety and speed.

Simone sat next to Ian in the back of the new SUV driven by another Trent Associate, Mike Bennett. Next to Mike was Trent Associate Austin Gable. Both bodyguards were ex-Marines and good guys whom Simone trusted. Despite the short notice, James had secured extra security. A state trooper led the way and behind them, in an unmarked sedan, a US marshal followed.

Johnny and Milo were checking out Ian's apartment. If they discovered the Dresden Group's files, they would send a copy via email. Ian checked his phone repeatedly for the email, but mostly, she was certain, for an update on his father.

Simone's heart constricted. If it were her father, she'd be doing the same. Ian's sentiment—*family always comes first*—resonated with her. It had to be why she'd agreed to this unpredictable detail.

Thankfully, Mike and Austin would accompany them to Bristle Township, and the sheriff's department would provide additional security while there. Simone didn't want to think about the fact that if anything happened to Ian, ultimately she would be responsible.

There was already one death on her conscience. She wasn't going to let there be another.

As the caravan approached an intersection, the light turned yellow. The state trooper in front of them brought his car to a halt. Mike braked, the SUV slowing.

"Incoming from the right!" Austin shouted the warning just as a beat-up, older brown pickup shot out of a side street straight at them.

Simone grabbed Ian with both hands, shoved him facedown on the seat between them and covered his body as best she could with her own.

Mike hit the gas and swerved around the back of the cruiser, but not before the oncoming truck hit the back end of the SUV, sending it spiraling. The crunch of metal twisting echoed through Simone's head with piercing clarity.

The brown truck careened to a halt in the middle of the street, its front end smashed, smoke and steam billowing out of the damaged engine.

Mike gained control of the SUV and brought it to a stop, facing the opposite direction. Both the state trooper and the marshal jumped out of their vehicles with guns drawn as they descended on the two assailants inside the pickup.

"Bogie on our six," Austin said, meaning a bad guy was behind them.

Mike stepped on the gas and sped down the street.

Simone turned to look out the back window. Sure enough, two motorcycle riders were bearing down on them. Each rider had an automatic machine gun in hand. The trooper and the marshal dove for cover.

Simone's heart jackknifed into her throat. Once again, she threw herself over Ian just as a barrage of bullets hit the back of the SUV, taking out the rear window.

"How did they find us?" Ian demanded, trying to rise.

Simone didn't have an answer, but something must've alerted them. Was it possible they knew Ian was under the protection of Trent Associates and had followed Mike and Austin to the safe house?

"We need to get out of this vehicle," she yelled to her coworkers.

Austin turned in the seat. "There's a parking garage up ahead. We'll enter and let you two out. Then we'll lead them away and send somebody to pick you up."

"Good plan," Simone said.

The SUV turned sharply into the parking garage, sending the interior of the vehicle into dim light. The tires squealed on the smooth surface as they took the curving ramp upward.

"Get ready," Austin said over his shoulder. "As soon as we get around this next corner, Mike will stop and you jump out."

Simone tapped Ian on the back. "Be ready."

"I am!" came his growled reply.

The SUV suddenly braked hard and screeched to a

halt. Simone was pitched against the front seat, the breath whooshing from her lungs. Shaking off the momentary discomfort, she tapped Ian on the shoulder again. "Out," she commanded.

He popped the rear door open and climbed out, keeping low. Simone scrambled across the bench seat and followed him. Slamming the door shut, she grabbed Ian's arm to propel him around the front end of a parked 4x4 where they crouched from sight. The SUV sped away, climbing higher into the parking maze.

The roar of two motorcycles filled the garage as the pair chasing them raced to catch up to the SUV.

Simone kept a hand on Ian's arm. "Wait. We need to make sure they are on the next level before we move."

Ian nodded. She was thankful he was calm. Some protectees would have panicked in a situation like this, but not Ian. His body was tense, his expression grim. Admiration and respect for him coursed through her.

The motorcycles had circled back, the rpms of the engines dropping as they slowed to an inching crawl toward them.

Simone's breath caught. "They're tracking us." She yanked her phone from her pocket, quickly powered the device off and removed the battery. "Your phone."

Ian frowned but handed it to her. She did the same with his phone then threw both devices over the railing behind them. A few seconds later they heard the phones shatter on the concrete.

The motorcycles stopped. The exhaust from the idling engines filled the air, stinging her nose. Their lack of movement only confirmed Simone's suspicion. The two assailants had been tracking one of their phones.

The seconds stretched as their pursuers waited.

One wrong move on her or Ian's part could draw attention to where they hid. Her legs ached. The need to move was like an itch she couldn't scratch. From Ian's grimace, he too struggled to remain frozen, waiting, barely able to breathe for fear the fumes would send either of them into a coughing fit.

Finally, the two bikers roared away. The resonance of their engines bounced off the concrete walls until there was only the sound of her and Ian's ragged breathing.

Frustration for not having ditched their phones earlier washed over her. She should have known someone savvy enough to hack the Delaney computer servers would be capable of tracking their cell phones.

Ian's distressed stare met hers. "We have to contact James."

Simone's instincts yelled no. Not until she had Ian somewhere safe. "I fear that whoever is after you not only tracked one of our phones, but they could have hacked the microphone and listened to our conversations. They, no doubt, know our plans."

His eyebrows dipped. "Then we need to change our plans."

"Exactly." Taking his big, surprisingly calloused hand, she led him to the stairwell. Their footsteps boomed off the concrete as they rushed down the stairs and came out on the backside of the parking structure.

The sidewalks were busy with pedestrians. The summer heat bounced off the pavement. "This way," she said.

"Where are we going?" Ian asked, keeping step with her.

"Back to the safe house." Then they could regroup and make a new plan.

The sound of approaching motorcycles sent Simone's

heart hammering against her rib cage. Jolted into action, she tugged Ian into a souvenir shop and moved to the back of the store, away from the windows. There was only so much she could control in this situation. She grabbed a navy baseball hat with a red B on the front and put it on Ian's head, then plucked a floppy white-straw hat off a rack for herself. "We need to change our appearance."

She pointed to a stack of men's T-shirts. "Find something that fits you."

"We'll look like tourists," he said.

"Yes, we will. And hopefully blend in with the autumn-leaf peepers who migrate through Boston to view the changing colors of the foliage." She gave him a little push. "Go. Hurry."

With a shake of his head, he picked through the shirts.

For herself, she grabbed a pair of summer capris and a lightweight blousy shirt. She darted into the dressing room. The shirt hid her holstered weapon nicely. Thankfully, she'd worn her black flats today.

Ian had chosen a light gray crew neck shirt with the word Boston in blue letters across the front. It stretched nicely across defined chest muscles that gave Simone a moment of pause. With a mental shake of her head for even noticing his physique, she nodded her approval.

She paid for their things and put their clothes in the big bag the clerk handed them.

"Here we go." She handed Ian the bag as they walked out onto the sidewalk. She enfolded his hand within her free one, leaving her other hand available to draw her weapon if needed. "Keep your head down and the brim low."

"Aye, aye, captain," Ian said, his voice gruff.

She smiled up at him. "We're just two tourists out on an afternoon walk to see the pretty trees of New England."

The warmth in his eyes sent her heart pumping. "If only that were the case."

She swallowed the sudden lump in her throat. An unexpected yearning took hold of her. A yearning to be a couple exploring a new city together, to take in the sights without a care in the world. To be in love. To be happy. But she didn't deserve happy because she'd failed her best friend, and she wouldn't allow herself to love Ian. Or anyone, for that matter. She'd only let them down in the end.

Up ahead, the entrance to Boston's Metro station loomed. There was more than one way to get to Colorado than a private jet.

"Come on," she insisted. "How do you feel about commercial flying?"

FIVE

The mad dash through the Boston transit system to only end up where they'd been headed in the first place, Logan Airport, left Ian frustrated and with a pounding headache. Simone kept his questions at bay with nothing more than a raised hand. She glanced around meaningfully, as if to point out they could be overheard. Okay, he got it. She was suspicious and maybe a bit paranoid. Not everyone was out to get him. At least, he prayed not.

But being cautious and guarded was part of her job. He couldn't imagine living with that kind of tension and constant wariness. He'd only been living with it for a short time and it was exhausting.

Instead of boarding the private jet that had brought him to Boston, Simone bought tickets on the first available plane to New York City. In coach, no less. He'd spent the hour-and-a-half flight with his knees jammed into his chest, making his back cranky.

At LaGuardia Airport in New York, he'd insisted on first-class tickets. There was no way he was going to suffer another two and a half hours bent like a pretzel. They barely conversed on the flight. Simone took the opportunity to rest, which he didn't begrudge her. He tried to do the crossword puzzle in the back of the airline magazine but couldn't concentrate. His thoughts bounced between worry for his father, curiosity about the woman sitting next to him and trying to remember what had sent him down this unexpected and dangerous road.

When they touched down at Denver International Airport, Simone hustled him off the plane ahead of the other passengers. Her take-charge attitude had people stepping aside without question. She was a force to be reckoned with. And he was fascinated. Not that he had any intention of letting that fascination morph into anything else.

He wasn't looking to become emotionally, or otherwise, involved with his bodyguard. Relationships were a hindrance to his orderly life that he wanted no part of. Risking one's heart for love meant opening oneself up for pain and torment if something should happen to the loved one. He'd rather go through life without that hazard.

As soon as they entered the terminal, the pre-paid cell phone she'd purchased during their layover in New York chirped. She'd already communicated with her boss so was expecting him to respond.

She looked at the message. "Mike and Austin are waiting for us out front with a rented vehicle."

Ian frowned and rubbed at the kink in his neck. "How did they get here before us?"

"They took the private jet out of Boston."

"Of course they did." He couldn't keep the snark out of his tone. Though he couldn't fault Simone for trying to throw off the people tracking him by taking the commercial flights rather than the expected private jet.

Simone cocked one eyebrow at him then led the way through the terminal to the underground train. As it made its way to the main exit, she kept herself between him and anyone else. If someone moved too close, she interceded by firmly asking them to step back. He could only grimace a silent apology in her wake. If the situation were different, he'd have found it comical with her in her flouncy top and capris bossing everyone around like a drill sergeant in boot camp.

Once past the point of no return to the main terminal without going through security screening, Simone's tension rolled off her like a rogue wave, ratcheting up his own anxiousness. She seemed to see a potential threat in every corner.

Through the glass double doors of the exit, Ian saw a white SUV idling at the curb, Mike standing by the back passenger door. Austin was no doubt in the driver's seat.

Ian wasn't looking forward to more sitting on the drive ahead to Bristle Township. What he needed was a good workout to loosen the kinks in his muscles.

They made their way toward the exit just as two men, both wearing green camo jackets, came through the doors and stepped right into their path. Simone wedged herself in front of Ian. One of the men, who looked to be in his early twenties with his scraggly beard and hunched shoulders, veered to the right.

The other, older man, tall and thick with a shaved head and brown eyes, scowled and lifted his hands as he halted and got in Simone's face. "Hey," he said. "Outta the way, lady."

"Move back!" Simone commanded.

The man put his hands on her shoulders and shoved her hard.

Simone reacted in a flurry of action. She pushed the man backward with both hands then sent a right jab to his nose.

Ian's instinct was to help Simone. He stepped forward, but movement in his peripheral vision caused him to falter. The younger man pivoted and lunged for Ian, one hand reaching out to grab him by the shirt.

Ian caught the glint of steel in the guy's hand and shifted to block the incoming series of stabs by using his forearm as a barrier against the hand holding the hunting knife. Stinging pain on his forearm barely registered as he fought to keep the weapon from sinking into his gut.

In this situation, Ian's height over the younger man wasn't an advantage. Ian had to bend at the waist to keep his arm low enough to block the knife. But thankfully, he had sparred enough with Nick and Alex in the family dojo for his brain to kick in.

He pinned the guy's knife hand to his side. Manipulating his hip as a fulcrum to spin the man, he used his free hand to punch his assailant in the head multiple times.

Then Mike and Austin were there, along with airport security. The knife-wielding man and his partner were subdued, hands zip-tied behind their backs and taken into custody.

Breathing hard from the adrenaline and exertion, Ian reached for Simone. "Are you okay?"

She shot him a concerned look. "You're bleeding!"

Grabbing his dress shirt from the bag with their clothes, she quickly ripped it into ribbons before wrapping several layers around his arm and tying it off. Blood seeped through the material.

"That's an expensive bandage," he muttered.

"You'll get over it," she retorted. "How did you learn to defend yourself against a knife attack?"

He shrugged. "Practice. When Nick and I were young,

our father hired a martial arts instructor to teach us how to defend ourselves. I've kept up the workouts."

"You did well." The words sounded reluctant, as if she hadn't wanted to say them.

High praise, coming from her. He'd never thought he'd actually have to use any of the martial arts moves in real life. Not even in the military had he needed to call upon his skills in anything but training situations. He sent a thankful prayer to God above for the knowledge. He'd also have to thank his father the moment he saw him. His gut twisted with worry. How was his dad doing?

While keeping pressure on the wound, Simone directed him to a bench just as medical personal joined them.

A medic knelt beside him, unwrapped the swathe of cloth and assessed the damage to his forearm. "This is pretty superficial. I'll use tape to close the wound. It could have been much worse."

After dressing the wound properly, the EMT explained signs of infection to watch for and advised Ian to see his primary doctor for additional care. Ian was then released to give his statement to the local police.

Once the two assailants—who'd both lawyered up right away—had been taken away by the police, Simone ushered Ian to the waiting white SUV outside. He and Simone slid into the back seat. Ian leaned his head against the headrest and closed his eyes as exhaustion settled over him like a shroud, making him wish he'd taken advantage of their flight to clock some sleep.

Austin pulled the rented SUV away from the curb.

Simone touched Ian's hand, drawing his attention as little zings of sensation shot up his arm. "I'm so sorry," she said. "I guess taking the long way around wasn't enough to keep the bad guys from finding you."

He dismissed the thrill of her touch to residual adrenaline. But he couldn't keep from curling his fingers around hers, if only to assure her he didn't blame her for what had happened. "Not your fault. They were waiting for us and would have attacked no matter when or how we arrived at the airport."

"I should've kept an eye on the little guy." The self-recrimination in her tone made Ian cringe. "The big guy was a distraction."

"You faced the immediate threat," Ian said. "You did your job."

She squeezed his hand and then let go, clearly intending to slip hers away. He held on, for some reason needing the connection, which was so unlike him. He filed the thought away and took satisfaction when her fingers curled over his.

They drove out of Denver, the city giving way to pine-covered forests and the rising mountains of the Rockies. Ian was always surprised by the beauty of the terrain. "I've been all over the world but there's something majestic about this place. I feel closer to God in the natural wonders of the Rocky Mountains."

"What brought you to Colorado?"

Simone's softly asked question drew his gaze. Her dark eyes held his captive. She was lovely in the afternoon light shining through the SUV's windows. Tendrils of hair had escaped her bun, softening her edges. He imagined in her line of work she had to stay sharp, intense and focused. His fingers itched to release the clip holding back her hair.

"My father wanted to relocate to a place that was remote but still in the United States," he answered. "I'm not sure why he didn't want to return to Ireland to live. We have land there." He shrugged. "I found the property in Bristle Township, and we built a new home."

"Why remote?"

A question Ian had asked Patrick on numerous occasions and had been frustrated by his father's dodgy answers. "I don't know. He said he wanted to be far from the memories of my mother, yet he insisted we build an exact replica of our Boston house."

"From all accounts, your father is a tad eccentric."

He let out a short laugh. "A 'tad' is an understatement. He's pulled some outlandish schemes."

"I heard about the treasure hunt," she said. "An interesting stunt for him to pull."

"A deadly one," Ian stated with some heat. Mention of the infamous quest set his blood to boiling. "I hadn't known what he was doing until it was too late to stop him."

Something Ian would regret forever. The hunt had cost lives, caused property damage and put a stain on the family name. Ian had worked to repair the destruction of the sheriff's department building and restore the Delaney honor, but there'd been nothing he could do about the people who'd lost their lives. It had been reckless of his father. Something Ian had never equated with Patrick Delaney until the last few years as age began to take its toll.

"We've got trouble on our tail," Austin said.

Ian stared out the back window. An extremely large pickup followed at a close distance. Its oversize stainless-steel push bar bore down on them, ready to ram the back end of the SUV.

Austin brought up the navigation system on the dashboard. "There's a back road coming up."

"Better for us to deal with this now," Mike said. He reached between his feet and came up with a wicked-looking automatic weapon.

Ian's gut clenched.

"Get us off this road," Simone said. "Then deal with it. We don't want any innocents hurt."

Even as the words left her mouth, the monster truck butted into their back bumper. The clash of metal against metal assaulted Ian's ears. The whole SUV shuddered with the impact. His heart jackknifed in his chest. He gripped the handle over the door to keep from being flung forward and braced his feet on the floorboard.

"I've got the pedal to the metal. I'm giving it all it's got," Austin said. "They must have a souped-up engine."

"Take the next right," Mike shouted, indicating a gravel drive just past a mailbox.

Austin cranked the wheel and the large SUV made the sharp turn onto the gravel road, rocks and debris flying from beneath the tires. The force of the turn flung Ian into the passenger door, and Simone slammed against his side.

She gripped his shoulder and looked him in the eye. "Keep your head down. No matter what."

His jaw clenched. "What are you going to do?"

"We're going on the offensive," she stated.

"Hang on!" Austin yelled. He yanked the steering wheel sharply, sending the SUV sliding into a circle and up onto the dirt alongside the road. Then he stomped on the brakes, bringing the SUV to a shuddering halt.

"Down!" Simone growled at Ian.

Heart pounding in his ears, he hunkered as best he could as she popped her door.

Mike opened the front passenger door and stood on the step rail of the SUV. Austin did the same. The three protection specialists riddled the monster truck with bullets as it barreled past. Ian clamped his hands over his ears against the onslaught of noise.

"Let's go!" Simone bounced into her seat next to Ian, slamming her door shut. He sat up and saw the truck veer off into the woods and disappear from sight.

The two bodyguards retook their seats, Austin stepping on the gas and heading back to the highway at breakneck speed.

"Keep your eyes sharp," Mike said, his head on a swivel as he searched for threats.

"And you—" Simone tugged on Ian's good arm. "Stay down. We're not out of danger yet."

By the time they arrived in Bristle Township, Ian's head throbbed and his arm stung. The over-the-counter pain medication the paramedic had given him had worn off. Blood seeped through the bandaging on his arm.

When they arrived at the hospital, Simone insisted a doctor look at Ian's wound before she would allow him to head to the critical care unit where his father was being treated. After downing more acetaminophen and with a new dressing, he was released with the admonishment to keep the wound clean.

When they stepped onto the eighth floor, they found Nick pacing outside their father's ICU room. "Ian. Finally." He rushed forward, his eyes going to the bandage on Ian's arm. "What happened?"

"We were ambushed at the airport," Simone told him. "They were waiting for us."

Simone didn't mention they'd also been targeted on the road, which Ian appreciated. No need to worry his family any more than necessary.

Nick pushed out a breath. "We're paying you to protect him."

"It's not her fault." Ian defended her automatically. He wouldn't let her take blame for something out of her control.

Simone slanted him a glance rife with an emotion he wasn't sure how to interpret.

"Tell me about Dad," Ian said, needing to keep the focus on why they were in the hospital.

"His lungs filled with fluid. Cardiogenic pulmonary edema." Nick ran a hand through his hair. "We have to pray there isn't any permanent damage to his lungs or his heart. His blood pressure was through the roof. He's in an induced coma."

Obviously, Ian wasn't going to get any information from his father about the Dresden Group, but right now that really wasn't his priority. "I want to talk to the doctor and make sure they are doing everything they can."

Nick tucked in his chin. "What do you think I've been doing? You're not the only one who can throw their weight around. The doctors here are good. They're doing all they can."

Ian pulled in a deep breath. Trusting his brother was something he was slowly learning to do after so many years of Nick's less than responsible ways. He no longer put his personal entertainments above the needs of others. Ian was having trouble getting used to this new and improved version of his younger sibling. He credited Kaitlyn and little baby Rosie with the change, however the need to control had a powerful pull that took all his self-will to push aside.

"Do you know anything about the Dresden Group?" Simone asked Nick.

Ian also wanted to know the answer.

Nick frowned. "Dresden. The name sounds familiar, but I can't place from where. Why? Are they the ones after you? And why are they trying to kill you?"

"I wish I had the answers." There was nothing but a big blank abyss where his memories should be.

Placing a hand on Ian's shoulder, Nick asked, "You still don't remember what you were doing before the chopper went down?"

Ian rubbed at his temple in frustration. "No." He explained discovering that the Dresden Group was the last thing he'd been working on at his office. That everything pertaining to the group now appeared to have been wiped from the company's servers.

Nick let out a slow whistle. "That's not good. Could it be the government trying to cover something up?"

Ian groaned. "You and your conspiracy theories. The government wouldn't come after me this way, would they? And why?" He struggled through the ache in his brain to remember something, anything, that would give him a clue. But there was only a void. He was going to need another dose of pain reliever soon. The one he'd just taken had barely scratched the surface of his headache.

Simone shook her head. "No, the government wouldn't. At least, not so publicly."

"That's reassuring," he mocked.

"I'm kidding."

Was she? Her deadpan expression was hard to read.

"You should go home, Ian. You look beat," Nick said. "Get yourself cleaned up and rest. There's nothing you can do."

"You're here," Ian asserted, not willing to be sent off so unceremoniously.

Nick's mouth twisted. "True that. There's nothing either of us can do now, except pray for the treatments to work and to wait for the call from the medical team telling us he's on the mend."

Ian swiveled to Simone. "I don't want my father left unprotected. If this does have something to do with the Dresden Group, then my father could be in danger, as well, if he knows anything."

"Let me talk to the guys," she said. "One of them can stay here and keep watch."

The tension tightening his chest eased slightly. "Thank you."

"It's what I'm paid for." She shot Nick a look then turned away as she produced her phone and called her team. She arranged for Mike to remain at the hospital to keep Patrick Delaney safe. Ian was grateful to the protection specialists for accommodating his request.

"Before we head home," Ian said as the three of them walked to the hospital exit, "I want to stop by the sheriff's office and find out what Alex has learned since we've been gone."

Simone halted abruptly, blocking his path. "No. The sheriff can come to you at the estate. This is not up for debate."

Nick grinned. "I like her."

Ian shot him a glare. "My going home equals putting you and your family in danger."

With a snort, Nick tucked in his chin. "You don't have

to worry. Need I remind you what happened at Christmas?"

No, he didn't. The family estate had been attacked by unscrupulous thugs working for a man responsible for the death of little Rosie's mother. The house had withstood the assault but not without damage.

"We've since put in more security measures. Reinforced the windows and doors," Nick told Simone. "I even have a brand-new, double steel-plated Humvee." He gestured to the sliding glass exit doors and the large green vehicle parked at the curb.

Clearly impressed, Simone nodded. "The perfect way to escort your brother home. We'll ride with you while Austin follows."

"I'll drive," Ian said, holding his hand out for the keys. "My vehicle."

"Yes, but I know how you drive," Ian said, falling back on old banter. "I'll get carsick."

Nick dangled the keys. "Small price to pay for safety." He walked away, whistling.

Simone touched Ian's arm. "Come along, let your baby brother help you."

"I'll never hear the end of this," Ian fairly growled as they climbed into the Humvee, but he had to admit he was grateful for Nick.

Talking his younger brother into coming to Colorado had been a feat. Nick's nomadic lifestyle had once concerned Ian. He'd never dreamed that Nick would acclimate to Bristle Township the way he had or that he'd find love with the fiery sheriff's deputy.

At least one of them had found happiness.

His gaze slid to the woman sitting beside him as Nick

drove up the long, windy mountain road. She met his gaze with raised eyebrows. He glanced away, wondering at the sudden longing pinging in his chest.

SIX

Simone clasped her hands in her lap to refrain from reaching out for Ian's hand the way he had grasped hers when they'd left the airport. The contact had been surprisingly soothing. Not that she needed comfort, but he apparently had because he'd hung on after she'd tried to withdraw. She chalked up the need for connection as nothing more than adrenaline-fueled nonsense.

Getting emotionally involved with her client was not professional. Her job was to protect Ian, not to start a romance that had no chance of blossoming. Her life didn't allow for any sort of attachment. Not that she wanted any. She only wanted to redeem her past mistakes and keep her charge safe.

It rankled her that Ian had been attacked at the hospital and then on the road to Bristle Township, as well as hurt on her watch. The incidents stirred the gnawing guilt she'd lived with for so long. And Ian's gracious words, telling her and his brother it wasn't her fault, only made her feel guiltier. If he'd blamed her, at least they'd be in accord with one another.

Ian leaned forward to talk to Nick. "Hand me your phone so I can call Alex."

"I'll call him," Nick volunteered.

"You're driving."

"Ever heard of Bluetooth?" Nick stated with a glance in the rearview mirror. The sound of the phone dialing filled the interior.

No doubt it was hard for Ian to let someone else take control. He had no choice but to sit back. However, as soon as the sheriff was on the line, Ian sat forward and directed the conversation in a loud voice. The sheriff promised to meet them at the estate right away.

After Nick ended the call, Ian captured her hand, warmth pressing into her palm and shooting up her arm. Pointing their joined fingers through the sunroof of the Humvee, he said, "Watching the clouds forming shapes across a bright blue sky, I'm reminded how great God is. And that He created Heaven and the earth and all living creatures."

She wanted to remind him that some of God's creations were monsters, but she couldn't find her voice as she stared at their joined hands. His so much bigger and stronger than she expected. Rough, not soft. The soothing sensations she'd experienced earlier wove through her, making her want to snuggle close. She glanced sideways, studying his whiskered jaw, the sharp angles and planes of his handsome face. A slow smile curved his lips as he shifted his gaze to her, the brown depths catching the sunlight coming through the pane of glass above them.

Her mouth dried. A low and pleasant hum threatened to dismantle the shields guarding her heart.

What was she doing? Holding hands with her protectee, gazing at the sky like they were on some kind of romantic date or something. This was so unlike her.

She disengaged her hand and scooted as far from him

as her seat belt would allow. Her eyes shot to Nick, thankful his attention was on the road ahead and not the rearview mirror. "God is great, but some of His creations not so much. Someone wants you dead, Ian. We can't forget that fact."

His expression darkened. "People would rather blame God for the bad in the world than accept that each of us has free will. To do good or bad."

Her brow furrowed as his words seared through her. "I don't disagree with you. But we all pay the price for others' choices."

"Or benefit from others' choices," he replied softly, his curious gaze probing at her.

"You're a glass-half-full kind of guy," she said. He could afford to be. Up until now, his life hadn't been touched by evil. "I'm more the glass-half-empty type."

"Then we are a good balance for each other."

Choosing not to reply to that loaded statement, she watched as Nick slowed the vehicle at the entrance to the Delancy grounds. They waited for the large wrought-iron gates to part before proceeding along a private road flanked by well-manicured shrubs and flowers. She glanced behind to make sure Austin, and no one else, made it through the gates before they closed.

The Humvee rolled to a stop in front of the stone steps leading to the front door of the estate. She was again struck by the palatial, castle-like facade. The limestone mansion stood proud amid the forest backdrop. The lowering sun glinted off myriad stunning windows. Having been inside the top of the turrets rising out of the roofline, she knew what a stunning view the Delaneys had of Bristle Township and the surrounding county.

She remembered what he'd told her about his family's

move here. "You chose well," she told Ian as he joined her on the steps.

Surprise flashed in his eyes. He glanced at his home with a shrug. "It's much too ostentatious for my taste."

She had to bite her tongue to keep from asking what was his taste. His preference in home style had nothing to do with protecting him.

Simone and Austin followed Nick and Ian inside, which was just as impressive as the outside. The marble floor gleamed. A wide staircase leading to the second floor boasted a wrought-iron railing similar to the gate out front. Beautiful classic paintings hung on the walls. There was no mistaking the Delaneys were people of wealth. Unlike her family, who were blue-collar all the way.

Thankfully, protecting the handsome CEO of Delaney Holdings wasn't dependent on them having similar backgrounds.

"I'm going to freshen up," Ian stated and climbed the stairs.

Austin planted himself by the front entrance and Simone watched Ian go, debating whether to follow or not. Logic told her he was safe here, but the memory of him fighting off his attacker was etched in her brain. He shouldn't have had to defend himself.

"He'll be fine," Nick said from behind her. "I doubt he'd want you in his space."

"I'll do what's necessary to keep him safe," she muttered. "Even invade his personal space."

"Like I said, I like you," Nick remarked. "I have from the first time I met you. I think you're just what Ian needs."

Not sure how to take his statement, she focused on her job. "These people after your brother are determined."

Leading the way to the study, Nick asked, "What is this Dresden Group?"

"We don't know. Delaney's CFO said it was some subsidiary that was put in place long before her time there."

Nick's mouth pressed into a line. "My father would know."

"That was Ian's thinking, as well," Simone said. She sent up a prayer that Mr. Delaney survived, not only to give them answers, but because his sons would be devastated if he didn't.

"Water?" Nick asked as he grabbed a bottle from a minifridge.

"Please."

She'd nearly drank the whole bottle of cool liquid by the time Ian entered the study, wearing a fresh shirt and slacks. No sooner had he cleared the doorway than there was a knock at the front door.

"I'll get it."

Simone recognized Kailtyn Lanz-Delaney as she passed by the study opening.

A few moments later, Kaitlyn escorted the sheriff, Alex Trevino, and Deputy Daniel Rawlings into the study.

"What do we know?" Ian asked without preamble, his regard intent on the sheriff.

"Not much more than we did before. There were no viable fingerprints on any of the helicopter wreckage. The security cameras at the airport had gone out earlier in the day for about fifteen minutes. We think that must be when the sabotage happened," Alex said.

"And we found nothing of use in Ian's office, except this." Simone held out the square sticky note with letters and numbers written across it. She handed it to Alex.

He shook his head. "This could be anything."

Kaitlyn took the paper and stared at it. "Ian, you have no idea what this is?"

"None. I don't recall writing it or what it means," Ian said, frustration evident in his tone.

Nick moved to put his arm around Kaitlyn's waist and looked at the note. "That's not your writing. Though you do write like Dad." He looked up at them. "That's Dad's code for longitude and latitude."

Glancing between Ian and the scrap of paper in Nick's hand, Simone's eyebrows hitched upward. "Longitude and latitude? There are too many letters and numbers. And they aren't in the right order."

"That's because it's encoded," Nick said.

"Encoded?" She'd never seen a code like that before.

Ian ran a hand through his hair. "What are you talking about, Nick?"

"Remember the treasure hunt?" Nick gave him an incredulous look.

There was a collective groan from Daniel, Alex and Kaitlyn. Simone had heard enough about the infamous hunt to know what havoc it had wreaked on the town and the citizens, especially the sheriff's department.

"Dad didn't want anyone to know what he was doing, including us," Nick said. "I only know about it because I stumbled across it one day. He wrote the latitude and longitude of the buried treasure in code. Just like this."

Ian groaned. "The treasure has already been found. So that's a useless clue. We're back to square one. Dad's the only one who can explain about the Dresden Group." His fists clenched at his sides. "Unless I can remember."

His frustration was nearly palpable. Simone wished

there was something she could do for him, but Ian's brain would either heal and remember or not.

"It might not be a dead end," Nick said. "This doesn't look like the same code as the one Dad wrote for the buried treasure."

Ian stared at his brother. "How so?"

"A while back, I was going through some papers of Dad's, trying to find insurance information. I found his file folder with all the details of the buried treasure, including the map, which he slowly shared with the world. But there was a code written on the back, and it looked similar to this. I think he wrote the coordinates down in case he forgot where he buried the box."

"I still have trouble picturing your father going out and burying treasure," Kaitlyn said.

"I'm sure Dad got Collins to do it," Nick replied, referring to the Delaney butler. "The man is loyal to a fault. He will do anything for my father."

"Maybe Collins would know what these coordinates lead to," Daniel said.

"And maybe he would even have information about the Dresden Group," Simone added. The sooner the mystery was resolved, and the threat neutralized, the sooner she could move on to another assignment. One far from the handsome CEO who did funny things to her insides.

"Worth asking." Nick walked to a small control panel attached to the study wall and pressed a button.

A few moments later, Collins appeared. A tall, older man with graying hair, he was dressed impeccably in black slacks and a white dress shirt. Simone had vetted the household staff the first time she'd come to the estate and rather liked the older man and his wife, Margaret, who made sure the house ran smoothly.

"Ian!" Collins rushed forward to embrace him. "I'm so glad to see you in one piece. Margaret and I have been so worried."

Ian accepted the man's brief hug. "Thank you, Collins."

"Collins." Nick drew his attention. "Take a look at this paper. Can you make sense of it?"

Collins regarded the writing with a frown. "It looks like one of your father's codes." Worry darkened his eyes. "How is Patrick?"

"We're waiting for the hospital to call with an update," Nick said. "Do you think you can decipher this code?"

Collins studied the paper. "Given some time, maybe. It would depend on what criteria Patrick was using. He loves riddles and puzzles, as you know."

"Have you heard of the Dresden Group?" Ian asked.

Simone hoped the man would have answers and was disappointed when he shook his head.

"I've heard the name, but I can't recall in what context," Collins said. "I don't know anything about a group. Are they singers, perhaps?"

Nick chuckled. "No. That's doubtful."

"Sorry I couldn't be of more help," Collins said.

"We don't even know if this Dresden Group has anything to do with the threat against Ian," Kaitlyn pointed out.

"True, but we can't rule them out," Simone stated. Until they knew more, she had to be on guard. Without a clear motive, everyone was a suspect.

Ian's gaze whipped to her. "What else could there be? It was the last thing I was working on and all traces of this group were wiped from our company servers. That has to be significant."

She didn't have an answer. And it wasn't her job anymore to figure out the why. She'd put her investigation days behind her when she'd left the Detroit PD. Her job now was only to protect. But solving the mystery of who and why someone wanted Ian dead nagged at her like an itch she couldn't reach.

"I can figure this out," Nick said, striding across the room and sitting at the desk. "Working on the assumption that this has something to do with your helicopter crash, let's start there." He opened a drawer and pulled out a map of the area.

They all crowded around the desk. Simone hung back until Ian turned to her and held out his hand, inviting her to join them. Pleased, though she really had no business getting involved with the mystery of the code or being thrilled that he wanted to include her, she stepped forward and squeezed in beside him. His warmth wrapped around her, invaded her personal bubble, while his musky masculine scent did funny things to her insides.

"First we flip the letters and numbers." Nick put pen to paper and wrote. "Numbers are the degrees."

"And the second set of numbers?" Daniel asked.

"Steps," Collins offered. "When your father buried the treasure, he counted out the steps from where the longitude and latitude points met."

"So you did help our father bury that treasure," Ian accused.

Collins winced. "Unfortunately, at the time, I had no idea what mayhem the treasure hunt would cause, and Patrick threatened to fire me, and Margaret, if we revealed any knowledge of the prize's whereabouts."

"That's in the past," Alex pointed out. "Let's concentrate on the present. The letters don't make sense."

"They would if you knew our father," Nick said. "The first letter for each set of numbers is your basic north, south, east and west."

"Then what does BSM stand for?" Daniel asked.

"Back side of mountain," Simone offered at the same time as Ian. They shared a brief smile.

"Bingo!" Nick pointed on the map to a section outside of Bristle Township. "I think this code leads to somewhere in this vicinity."

"A few miles from where Ian's helicopter went down," Alex said.

"I must have been flying over the area to check out what was going on at that location," Ian said.

Kaitlyn put her hands on the desk. "That really doesn't make any sense, because you wouldn't have been able to see what was going on at ground level."

Ian looked at her. "I don't know what I was thinking." He looked to Alex. "I don't know why I didn't go straight to you with whatever sent me flying that day."

"Because you never think anyone is as capable as you," Nick offered.

Ian shot his brother a scathing glare.

"Well, there's nothing we can do about it now," Alex said. "Lamenting does no one any good. We need to focus on finding out what's going on here." Alex tapped the map.

"I'll go check out the area," Daniel said.

"Not by yourself," Kaitlyn said. "I'll go with you."

Nick's response was a quick, "No!"

"Why not?" She braced her fist on her hip, emphasizing the roundness of her belly.

Nick made a pained face. "Do I really have to answer that?"

Kaitlyn wrinkled her nose and turned to Alex. "Sheriff?"

Alex shook his head. "I have to agree with Nick. I'll go with Daniel."

Heaving a clearly frustrated breath, Kaitlyn said, "Leslie could go with Daniel."

Simone hadn't vetted anyone by that name. "Who is Leslie?"

"Leslie Quinn, a good friend," Kaitlyn said. "She rode on the volunteer mounted patrol and recently became peace officer standards and training certified after graduating from the Denver police academy."

Daniel shook his head. "No way. She would never agree to go if she knew I was going. Besides she's not..." He grimaced.

Kaitlyn's eyebrow quirked. "Not on the force yet?" She turned to Alex. "And just why is that?"

"I was giving her time to make sure joining the sheriff's department was what she really wanted," Alex said.

"I think graduating top of her class and then coming back here and asking you for a job pretty much ensures that becoming a deputy is what she wants. Besides, we are a deputy down. Make her a deputy unofficially until the official paperwork can be taken care of. This solves everybody's problem."

"Speak for yourself," Daniel moaned.

"Just because you two have history doesn't mean you can't work together," Kaitlyn said. "Does it?"

Alex also turned his gaze to Daniel.

He drew himself up. "Of course, we can work together."

"I'll call her as soon as I leave here," Alex said.

Kaitlyn rubbed her hands together, clearly pleased. "Leslie knows this mountain better than any of us."

"Can't argue with that," Daniel muttered.

"As fun as this little in-house drama is," Ian said, "let me make this very clear. I'm going."

Simone's response was just as quick as Nick's had been. "No. You are not leaving the safety of the estate."

"I appreciate you wanting to protect me, but I am going to see this through." Ian's tenor was unyielding. "I'll not hole up here like some scared rabbit waiting for the fox to pounce."

"I don't want your appreciation, Ian," Simone ground out through clenched teeth. "I need your cooperation if I'm to do my job."

"Then you'd best come with me to keep me safe." There was a challenge in his tone.

Frustration clawed up her spine. At every turn, this man was a challenge. He couldn't just do as he was asked and lie low. He had to be in charge, taking risks, making her life difficult.

"Hold on," Alex said, drawing everyone's attention. "No one is going anywhere just yet. It will be dark soon. And we need a plan. There are no roads leading into this area."

"ATVs?" Nick suggested. "We have two."

Daniel shook his head. "The forest is too thick for motor vehicles. Only way in is on horseback."

Surely that would deter Ian from thinking he could go trekking through the woods looking for trouble.

"That works for me," Ian said.

Simone barely refrained from rolling her eyes. "You ride?"

"I do." He had the gall to look offended by her question. "I've played polo most of my adult life."

"Of course you have." She scoffed. "Not quite the same type of riding."

"I know how to control a horse whether on the pitch or on the trail."

She held up a hand. "Pitch?"

"The polo field." He pointed to her. "What about you? Do you know how to sit a horse?"

"Yes, as a matter of fact, I do. I was horse crazy as a teen. I spent many summers at horse camp learning how to take care of and riding horses."

"Good. Then it's settled. We'll both go."

"Excuse me?" How did he come to that conclusion? "Just because we can doesn't mean we should."

"If you're not up for it…" He shrugged.

The man was so irritating, and so stubborn, Simone wanted to scream. "Do you have horses here?" She already knew the Delaneys didn't have stables.

Ian paused and then turned to Alex. "Where do we get horses?"

"As much fun as it has been to watch you two spar…" Alex's amused gaze bounced between Simone and Ian.

Heat crept up her neck and into her cheeks. Had she really just argued with Ian like that in front of everyone? How much more unprofessional could she be? It was Ian's fault, she decided. The man rattled her composure and made her lose sight of decorum. She needed to get a grip.

Alex continued. "Ian, you and your bodyguard are staying put."

Gratitude flooding her, Simone inclined her head in acknowledgment and slanted a look at Ian to see his reaction.

His jaw firmed and a mutinous gleam entered his dark eyes.

Uh-oh. She had a feeling derailing Ian's plans would be like pushing a square rock up a steep mountain. But thwart him she would. Even if that meant camping outside his door to make sure he didn't sneak off in the middle of the night to go exploring in the woods.

SEVEN

Unbelievable. A prisoner in his own home. Ian paced the length of his suite. How had he let this happen?

He pounded a fist against his thigh. His life was spinning out of his control.

Logically, it was the safest thing for everyone for him to stay put inside the estate. But it abraded his sense of responsibility. This was his problem to solve. He wanted to be out there tracking down the person who was trying to kill him and find out why. What had brought this on? What bad thing had he done to someone that they would want him dead?

He closed his eyes and tried to visualize that last day in his office, but there was nothing there. No memory of what the Dresden Group files contained. No memory of leaving the office and flying across the country to Colorado. And no memory of what had sent him up in the air in his helicopter. Getting out there himself might be the only way he would remember.

He needed to talk some sense into the sheriff. Alex's deputy wouldn't even know what he was looking for. But Ian would once he was there, wouldn't he? Going into the woods surely would jog his memory.

Yes, he was going to call the sheriff and demand to go with the deputy into the woods. With determined steps, he searched his room for his phone, then remembered with a groan that Simone had demolished it back in Boston. He'd have to use the house phone in the study. He opened his door and stepped out into the hall.

"Going somewhere?"

He froze, the hairs along his nape shivering at Simone's sultry voice. He slowly turned. Light from the wall sconce glowed softly over her. She'd changed back into her pantsuit. She looked every inch the professional bodyguard that she was. But she was so much more. She was kind and caring. Intelligent, with a strength of character that he respected. "What are you doing?"

"I didn't think you'd stay in your room all night." She stepped closer, bringing with her a floral scent. Her skin appeared fresh. Her lips rosy. "What are you doing?"

It took a second for her words to penetrate the haze of attraction spinning around him. Did he fess up and tell her exactly what he was going to do? He heaved an agitated breath. No, he wouldn't. She would never let him leave. And Alex would never agree to let him accompany the deputy. Best to accept that, for now, he was trapped for his own good. "I'm headed to the dojo."

"I'll go with you."

His chin dipped. "You plan to watch me work out?"

She shrugged, the movement a delicate gesture that belied the power he knew she carried. "If that's what it takes to make sure you don't do anything foolish."

His defenses rose. "Why would you think I'd do something foolish?"

"Because, believe it or not, Ian, I've guarded a lot of men like you. Men who think they are in control and should be able to manipulate and maneuver every situation to meet their satisfaction. But that is not going to happen on my watch."

Irritation that she'd lump him in with some nameless men, whom she apparently held in disdain, raced along his limbs and heated his face. He didn't like the truth in her words. He was used to having life and circumstances bend to his will. But not this time. He had no control, no moves to make that would ensure a successful outcome. Ian had never been in a situation like this before. He'd never had his life threatened, nor had he ever had to relinquish his freedom to someone else. And he didn't like the way it made him feel vulnerable and out of sorts.

"I really don't want an audience while I work out." He walked away, heading for the dojo built into one of the lowest-level rooms of the house. His father had insisted he and Nick be proficient in defending themselves if the need should ever arise. Skills Ian had never thought he'd have to call upon as a civilian.

"Too bad." She stayed right on his heels.

He stopped abruptly. She ran into him, her softness bumping up against him, creating a firestorm of electricity that coursed through his veins. He pivoted to stare at her. "The only way I'll let you in the dojo is if you spar with me." He kept the corners of his mouth from curling, confident there was no way she'd take up the challenge.

"I would," she quipped back, "but I don't have any clothes appropriate for sparring with you."

"Oh, I can fix that," he replied, wanting to see just how far she'd take this gambit. "I'm sure something of Kaitlyn's would fit you."

He strode to the laundry room and opened a cupboard filled with folded clean clothes. He picked a pair of Kaitlyn's non-maternity sweatpants and one of her long-sleeved T-shirts. "I'm sure my sister-in-law won't mind if you borrow her clothes. Here, try these."

In the brightness of the overhead light, he could see Simone's misgivings as she accepted the clothes. "I don't think this will be a good idea."

"Maybe not," he said. "But it's the only way you're getting into the dojo."

She narrowed her gaze. "I'll wait outside the dojo doors."

He should be glad she'd backed down, but he couldn't stop the bubble of disappointment. Or the words that came out of his mouth. "There is a window I could escape through."

For some reason, it was important to him that she accept his challenge. Not that he intended to hurt her in any way. But he wanted her to know he didn't need a babysitter. That he could take care of himself. If he were honest with himself, he wanted more of her praise. And that was so ridiculous, it was laughable. Since when did he ever crave anyone's approval?

Simone gave a short laugh that was anything but amused. "Fine. Let's go."

Heart jumping, he led the way to the dojo. With each step, misgivings assaulted him. What was he doing? Challenging her to some kind of duel? Of all the senseless things... What did he hope to accomplish? But he couldn't back down now. He'd never backed down from a challenge. Ever.

Gesturing to the restroom next to the dojo, he said, "You can change in there."

She hesitated. He held his hands up, palms out. "I promise I won't skip out the window."

"I'll hold you to that promise."

"I never break my promises." He gave her a sharp nod then went inside the dojo. He prowled the space like a caged animal, his senses firing and his mind reeling. Were they really going to spar?

A few minutes later, she joined him. The sweatpants were a bit short, but they'd do. She'd pushed up the sleeves of the T-shirt and tucked the hem into the waistband of the sweats.

Dragging his gaze from how cute she looked, he went to the sound system and turned the music on. He liked to work out to the sultry sounds of South America. There was something about the Latin rhythms and melodies that stirred him in ways most other music did not.

"Interesting choice of music," she commented.

Suddenly unsure of himself, he shrugged off the uncomfortable self-consciousness. "I like the beat. We'll warm up first." He positioned himself in the middle of the mat-covered floor. "I do fifty jumping jacks, fifty push-ups, fifty sit-ups and fifty lunges on both legs, before anything else."

She inclined her head. "Bring it on."

Of course, she was confident. The woman was in good shape and had no problem keeping up with his pace. By the time they'd completed the warm-up, sweat dripped down his back. Simone was amazingly light on her feet, barely making any sound on the rubberized mats. She appeared hardly winded by the vigorous exercise.

"Hand-to-hand or do you want to use weapons?" he asked, curious to see what she'd prefer.

She glanced at the rack of martial arts equipment. "Sticks. Less chance of physical contact. I wouldn't want to get sued for assaulting you."

He barked out a laugh. "I'm not the suing type. But sticks it is." He tossed one of the long, blunt-ended wooden staffs to her, which she deftly caught, and took a ready stance. Interesting choice. The use of sticks often mimicked empty-handed strikes, the stick becoming an extension of one's self.

Mirroring her, he nodded. "Begin."

At first, their strikes were tentative; they each seemed to be testing one another. Ian was impressed by how well she handled the staff. Soon, the sparring turned more determined, more forceful. The sound of the wooden sticks clashing together nearly drowned out the music.

He managed to sweep her legs, toppling her over. He didn't take any joy in the momentary victory. She bounded to her feet in a swift move that was both surprising and impressive. Then she was attacking with more vigor, forcing him into a corner. Ian bumped up against the wall. Her stick pressed at his throat, the pressure not painful, but she was clearly making a point that if she wanted, she could render him unconscious.

"Want to call it?" she asked, her warm stare filled with challenge.

His eyes dropped to her upturned mouth as her breaths came out in little puffs. Her cheeks held a rosy hue from the exertion. She was beautiful and exciting and oh, so off-limits. But what he wanted, more than anything, was to kiss her. Fully. Deeply.

She moistened her lips. An invitation?

His gaze rose to meet hers. The spark of attraction he felt was reflected in her gorgeous eyes. He leaned forward, expecting her to back away. Instead, she rose on tiptoe, bringing her mouth closer as she decreased the pressure on the stick.

Mind reeling, he told himself he shouldn't kiss her. It wouldn't be wise, practical, or responsible. But in this moment, he didn't want to do the right thing. He wanted to do the dangerous thing. She wasn't a physical threat, but she was a danger to his heart.

Unable to resist, he lowered his head. Their lips met. If he had expected her to be soft and yielding, he was wrong but not disappointed. She kissed him back with the same sort of invigorating energy she did everything else. Sensations ran rampant within him as the world faded to this moment in time.

A loud, intrusive knock and the discreet clearing of a throat jolted through him.

They broke away from each other, breathing hard, holding their sticks at the ready toward the threat standing in the doorway.

Collins.

Ian relaxed his stance.

Simone walked to the rack and set her stick in its place, keeping her back to them.

"Sorry to interrupt," Collins said. "But the night-duty nurse from the hospital wants to talk to you on the house phone in the study."

Simone whipped around to stare at the man. "What?"

Ian frowned, dropped his stick and moved toward the door. "Why didn't she call Nick?"

"She asked for you." Collins matched his pace as he bounded up the stairs to the main floor. "She would only talk to you. She was quite insistent."

Aware Simone followed closely, Ian entered the study and grabbed the receiver off the desk. "This is Ian Delaney."

"Mr. Delaney, this is Janice Wheeler. I'm your father's night nurse. He's awake and asking for you."

His hand tightening around the phone, so many emotions and thoughts coalesced through Ian. His father was awake and asking for him. Did that mean Dad was going to be all right? Would they finally have the answers about the Dresden Group? Heart jumping in his throat, Ian said, "We'll be right there."

"Not 'we,'" Janice quickly replied. "I'm sorry, Mr. Delaney, but only one person is allowed to visit. It would be better if just you came. Quickly."

Ian hesitated, flicking his gaze to Simone. A deep frown marred her pretty brow. He turned away from her. "I have to let my family know." Nick would never forgive Ian if he didn't tell him what was happening.

"Please, your father wants it to be just you. He insisted that no one else be informed that he was awake. He can be quite persuasive."

Ian knew only too well how Patrick Delaney could manipulate and persuade anyone to do whatever he wanted. He was a man used to getting his way.

Annoyed but anxious for the answers to the mystery of the Dresden Group and to see for himself that his father was okay, Ian would risk his brother's hurt feelings. "I'll be right there." He hung up.

Simone stepped in front of him. "Excuse me? You'll be right where?"

He relayed what the nurse had said. "This is our opportunity to discover what he knows about the Dresden Group."

"No way," Simone said. "I'll call Mike and have him ask your father about Dresden."

Ian shook his head. "You don't know my father. He won't talk to a stranger about family business." And because he was well aware Simone wouldn't let him go anywhere without her, he added, "We need to go. You and me."

She seemed to consider his words. "All right. But we take Austin with us."

"I'd rather he stay here to protect my family." He narrowed his gaze, purposely challenging her. "Unless you don't think you can protect me." He hated poking her with the jab, but he needed to go, quickly, and with as little fuss as possible.

Her lip curled. "I can protect you. Unless you'd rather wait until the sheriff can accompany you, since you seem to respect him."

Ian frowned. This wasn't about respect. "Fine. We'll take Austin with us." Ian turned to Collins. "Please don't say anything to Nick. I don't want to hurt him. I'll explain to him when I come back."

A pained grimace crossed the older man's face. "But what if he asks where you all went?"

"Stay away from Nick and Kaitlyn as long as you can until morning. Though, honestly, we'll probably be back by then."

Simone turned to Collins. "Do you have the keys to the Humvee?"

"I do, as a matter of fact."

"Good. I'll go collect Austin and we'll meet you outside." Her gaze whipped to Ian. "If you leave without us, we will just follow you."

"I'm not going anywhere without my shadow," he stated.

After a very pointed glare, she headed for the hallway.

Did she really think he'd sneak away without her? Annoyed that he cared what she thought, he called after her. "And just for the record, I do respect you, Simone."

Her steps faltered and then, with renewed vigor, she hurried away.

Not only did he respect her, he admired her and was beginning to care about her in ways he'd not expected. And wasn't sure he wanted. She was prickly and, obviously, held him in disdain. Yet affection curled through him, filling him with a strange sort of hopeful dread he couldn't explain.

Simone hoped the call from the hospital meant Patrick Delaney was recovering. If he was awake, why hadn't Mike called? On her way upstairs, after changing into her pantsuit and putting her hair up in a bun, she dialed his cell phone, but it went to voice mail. An uneasy feeling bloomed in the pit of her gut. She called the hospital and checked to see that Janice Wheeler was actually on duty. Janice was one of the nurses Simone had vetted when she'd first arrived while Ian was unconscious.

The woman was on duty, but was with a patient and unable to come to the phone at the moment. Despite the confirmation, Simone couldn't shake the apprehension slithering up her spine. The sensation settled in the back of her throat.

She found Ian and Austin waiting by the front door. Ian had changed out of his sweats into dark-colored denim pants, athletic shoes and a lightweight sweater beneath a down parka. This casual look appealed to Simone. She gave herself a mental shake and accepted the warm jacket Ian handed her, no doubt one of Kaitlyn's, and hustled Ian into the Humvee without the rest of the household noticing.

She tossed Austin the keys as she slid into the back passenger seat, alongside Ian. His masculine scent, a heady combination of man and musky aftershave, reminded her of their time in the dojo. She'd been surprised by his skills. He'd claimed to practice, but she hadn't expected him to be so proficient. He could definitely hold his own, as she'd seen at the airport. She hadn't given him an inch though she'd anticipated she'd have to tamp down her own skills to match him.

And that kiss.

Wowee. Combustible. Unexpected. And totally inappropriate. She'd never been remotely attracted in a romantic way to a client. Maintaining a professional distance had served her well in the past. For some reason, Ian made keeping the walls up irritatingly difficult.

Yet she struggled to regret the moment.

Regretted or not, she would have to make sure there was no repeat. Kissing the man she was protecting violated her sense of propriety and wasn't good business practice. However, she couldn't deny that several of her Trent Associates coworkers had fallen for their protectees. But she had no intention of joining their ranks.

As the Humvee rolled silently down the driveway, Simone could feel waves of tension coming off Ian. No doubt, he was concerned about his father and the answers he might have regarding the Dresden Group. Her own curiosity was at an all-time high. That would do her no good. She wasn't there to solve a mystery. She needed to keep a clear head about the situation. No matter what they learned from Patrick, her job was to keep Ian safe.

Did he really respect her as much as he claimed?

Her heart thumped against her rib cage. She could feel a softening deep inside, unfamiliar and unwanted. Affection was blossoming and curling through her. She pulled her professional cloak around her like a shield.

"When we get to the hospital, we'll all enter together, but you and I will hang back to let Austin make sure this isn't some kind of trap."

From the front seat, Austin said, "I've been trying to get hold of Mike but he's still not answering. I've got a bad feeling about this. We should turn around."

Austin's words reinforced her own misgivings about this trip to the hospital. "Agreed."

"No! Don't you dare," Ian said promptly. "Press on. We're literally in an armored vehicle. How much safer could we be?"

Austin deferred to her. "Simone?"

Ian was right about the vehicle. Even if someone shot at them, the bullets wouldn't penetrate. But she couldn't be sure that once they arrived at the hospital she'd be able to keep Ian safe. And if Mike was in trouble, they'd need to help him. She was torn between her duty to Ian and her coworker.

Sending up a prayer that she wasn't making a mistake, she said, "Let's get to the hospital. We'll decide what to do once we arrive."

But the closer they drew to town, her qualms increased. She dug her cell phone out of her pocket to call the sheriff's department. "I don't have service."

"Me, neither," Austin said. "I did a second ago. This is weird."

Were their cell signals being jammed? Was someone using RFID to block cell transmission from a distance? At the thought of a radio frequency identification device, a sense of urgency battered at Simone. "Turn around."

"As soon as I find a turnout, I will," Austin said.

Ian bristled. "No, we are not turning around. My father's awake and asking for me. He'll have answers. Don't you want this over?"

Of course she did, but not at his expense. Something was wrong. She never should have allowed Ian to talk her into letting him leave the estate.

A loud bang echoed through the interior of the Humvee. The vehicle shuddered and rocked.

"What's happening?" Ian asked as the vehicle slowed.

"Whatever it is, it's not good." Simone leaned forward. "Don't stop!"

"I'm not. I have the gas pedal floored," Austin said, his voice holding a note of alarm. "I think we ran over a spike strip."

Simone's instincts had been right. This was a trap. Somebody had laid a strip of spikes across the road that had punctured the Humvee's tires.

"Keep going," she said. "I'm sure the tires are run-flats. We can at least get to the edge of town, then we can bail."

"I see movement behind us." Austin's tone was grim.

Fear shot through Simone. She turned around in her seat. There were no headlights, but with the brightness of the moon, there was no mistaking they were being followed. She could identify the outline of two large pickups bearing down on them, taking up both lanes.

"There's more!" Austin yelled.

In front of them, parked facing them and blocking both lanes of the road, were two more big trucks. Suddenly the darkness turned as bright as day when the trucks' glaring headlights switched on.

Austin slammed the brake, throwing her and Ian forward against their seat belts, then the vehicle was spinning as he cranked the wheel, taking the Humvee off the road. The seat restraint dug into Simone's chest as she hung on, praying for God's protection. Beside her, Ian pressed against her, his hands braced on the back of the front seat.

The Humvee bounced over rutted dirt before the earth gave way to air.

Simone's stomach wedged in her throat as Austin drove off a ledge.

Ten feet below, the Humvee landed upright with a jolt that rattled her teeth. Picking up speed, the vehicle careened down the side of a ravine, the headlights creating round glimpses of the forest. The front end glanced off the thick trunk of a lodgepole pine, sending the vehicle sliding sideways.

Despite the dizzying sensation, she threw a protective arm against Ian. At the same moment, he reached to brace her as the vehicle tipped over. The sound of metal crunching all around her reverberated through her head, and the seat belt bit into her lap, chest and shoulder. Then they were still as they came to a rest at the bottom of the ravine upside down.

EIGHT

Ian groaned. He was alive.

Simone's heart thumped against her ribs. Spiraling relief coursed through her veins. She gently shook him. "Ian."

His eyelids slowly opened. "Are you okay?"

She nearly cried that his first thought was of her. The man continued to surprise her and endear himself to her in ways that scared her and delighted her. And created pressure in her chest. "I'm a little banged up, but I'm okay. You?"

"The same."

She glanced up the hill and could see the bright lights of the monster vehicles shining down on them like vultures.

As if to punctuate her thought, gunfire rained down on them, but the Humvee held, the bullets making pockmarks in the reinforced windows and denting the armored frame.

"Austin!" Simone yelled.

His arms hanging limp, Austin didn't move or make any noise. She sent up another quick prayer. *Please don't let him be dead.*

This was her fault. She'd failed to protect them, just as she'd failed her friend all those years ago.

They couldn't just stay here waiting for the men with guns to come finish the job. Shaking off the memories threatening to pull her into a dark place, Simone undid her seat belt, sliding onto the ceiling of the Humvee. She maneuvered until her feet were under her in a crouch. She turned to Ian. "Can you reach your seat belt buckle?"

"Yes."

She grabbed his shoulders. "Do it. I've got you."

The click of the buckle releasing filled her ears and then he was sliding into her arms, his feet coming down hard on the ground where the open roof rested. His head landed on her knees before he was able to position himself upright into a squat beside her.

She reached forward to check Austin for a pulse, bracing herself for the worst. She laid two fingers against his neck. His pulse throbbed weekly. A wave of relief hit her. He wasn't dead. *Thank you, Jesus.* She needed to get him out of there. But how?

Austin was pinned by the steering wheel, the deflated airbag hanging as limply as Austin's arms. Had he been knocked unconscious by the force of the airbag deploying? Blood smeared his face, no doubt from a broken nose. She shook him gently. "Austin."

He groaned.

"I'm sure there's a tire iron in here," Ian said. "We can leverage it under the steering wheel carriage and lift it off of him."

"No," Austin ground out, his eyes opening. "Go. You're sitting ducks here. Get Ian to safety. Head through the forest toward town."

Simone's heart lurched with dread. "Austin, we can't leave you."

"I'll only be dead weight to you, and then all of us will die. Stay on mission, Simone. You know what you need to do."

She'd never been faced with this situation before. And had always thought she would do what she'd been taught as they'd often practiced for scenarios like this in training. James always said the protectee was the main objective. But how could she leave a man behind?

"No, we're not leaving you." Ian grabbed her arm. "We're not leaving him. That's not how it works. We have to make a stand. Let me have his sidearm."

"Listen to me," Austin rasped, clearly in pain. "If you run, it'll take them away from here. Lead them into the forest toward town. Then send help."

The sound of the men crashing down the side of the hill, coming closer with each ticking second, urged Simone to do the hard thing. As much as it broke her heart, she had to stay on task. Her objective was to keep Ian safe. She couldn't let him die. Then all of this would have been for naught.

She reached past Ian and opened the opposite side door. "Go!" She pushed at him. "We have to go!"

Ian stumbled from the vehicle and then pulled her out.

"Stay low," she told him.

Together, they ran into the forest. The gunmen's shouts echoed behind them.

Ian grabbed Simone's hand to keep from separating in the dark as they ran deeper into the forest. They stumbled over roots and barely missed trees appearing before them like specters. Branches snagged at their clothes, scratched at their skin. The earthy scent of moss and dirt filled his nostrils. Fear that he might be the cause of Simone's and Austin's deaths burned in his lungs.

Behind them, the sounds of men thrashing through the trees and calling to one another spurred Ian to move faster, but he had no idea where they were headed. Away from town or toward it?

He pulled Simone behind a large bramble bush. They crouched, catching their breaths.

"What are you doing?" she whispered. "We have to keep going."

The sky above them was obscured by a thick canopy of evergreen branches. "Going where?" He couldn't keep the frustration from his tone. "We don't even know what direction we're heading."

"Away from them." She pulled out her phone and hissed through her teeth. "No service."

"It's not normal. You should be able to get a signal," he said. "Could they be using a jamming device? I've read about that happening."

"They could. These guys are coordinated and sophisticated," she said. "Like soldiers."

Ian's gut twisted. "I've never heard Alex mention any military activity in Bristle County."

"Doubtful he knows, or I'm sure he'd be monitoring them. It could be a paramilitary group hiding in the forest," she said.

"Could that be what I'd discovered?" The thought ran rampant through his brain, but it didn't stir any memories. What would some militia group have to do with Delaney Holdings or the Dresden Group?

Simone tugged at him. "We have to go."

"Wait," he said as she started to rise. "We need to find a clearing where I can see the sky."

"The sky?"

"Yes. I can navigate by the stars."

She blew out a breath. "First meadow we come to, we'll stop."

Her grim sarcasm made him wince as they took off again, blindly running through the forest. They broke into a small clearing where the trees were spaced farther apart. He pulled her down into the tall grass swinging in the slight night breeze.

He pointed to the sky. "We have to find the Big Dipper, which will point us to the North Star. Once we do that, we'll know which direction to head."

She scooted so that they were back-to-back. "You're the expert, you find them. I'll keep watch." She held her weapon at the ready.

Admiring her strength and courage, Ian searched the sky, finding the Big Dipper. He followed the two point stars in what would be the ladle and drew an imaginary line to Polaris, the North Star, as most people called it.

"There. North is to our left." He kept his voice low.

"And how does that help?" she whispered back.

"The town is southwest of our estate. We need to head off in that direction." He gestured with a pointed finger.

"Go figure." Admiration laced her words. "Let's do it."

As they ran, careful to keep to the trees for cover, he couldn't deny how much her approval meant to him, even as guilt ate at him. Either the nurse had called to draw him into a trap, or the bad guys had been watching the estate for an opportunity, which he'd given them. Either way, this was on him. He raised a silent prayer, telling

God he would do whatever it took to keep Simone safe and asking Him to spare Austin.

As they stumbled along, Ian took every opportunity to check the sky to make sure they were running in the right direction.

A noise he could only identify as a car passing on asphalt echoed in his ears. He skidded to a halt and grabbed Simone's hand. "Do you hear that?"

"Yes. The road."

"This way." He steered them slightly off course toward the highway. They had made a big loop. "We know if we follow this road, it will lead us straight to town."

"We should stay to the trees."

"Agreed." Darting from tree to tree, they followed the road for what seemed at least a mile.

Headlights from behind them brightened their world as two vehicles rolled down the road, side by side. His adrenaline spiked as he glimpsed two of the trucks that had ambushed them earlier.

Simone yanked him behind a tree and into a low crouch. Ian wrapped his arms around Simone and hugged her tight, hoping to make them as invisible as possible. She shifted in his embrace so that her back pressed against his chest, her weapon held in front of her.

His warrior was always ready for battle.

Before he had time to analyze that wayward thought, the trucks drew abreast of them and inched their way forward. A wide beam of brightness from a search light mounted on one of the vehicles swept the side of the road.

"Don't move." Simone's voice was hardly audible. "Let them pass."

He held his breath, praying with all his might that

the trucks would head to town, thinking they'd already made it to safety.

Minutes ticked by. The cool night air seeped through his sweat-dampened shirt. His legs protested the prolonged squatting position, but he held steady, barely daring to breathe until the light moved on.

After several more excruciating minutes, Simone broke free to peer around the tree. "All clear."

Painfully, he stood and joined her as they watched the red taillights of the trucks disappear around a curve in the road.

"That was close," he breathed. His heart hammered in his chest and his blood pounded in his ears. His shook out the numbing sensations in his legs.

"Come on." Simone strode forward with purpose, still keeping to the trees.

From behind him, the sound of tires on asphalt jolted his heart. He pressed Simone up against a tree.

"Wha—"

"Shh," he hissed into her ear.

There was only darkness around them, but he was confident in what he'd heard. He dropped his forehead to the rough bark of the tree over Simone's head.

"Ian?"

"There were four trucks that ambushed us," he whispered. "Two went by. The other two must be following at a distance without their lights."

In a swift move, she reversed their positions so that she was shielding him. "This isn't good."

For a long heartbeat, he thought maybe the additional trucks had rolled past as he strained to listen. But then two sets of headlights burst on with a bright glow that made Ian cringe. He prayed they wouldn't be seen.

Suddenly the world around them turned even brighter. The two trucks that had passed earlier approached from the opposite direction, their headlights mingling with those of the other trucks.

Simone groaned. "They must have spotted us. Our only option is to go deeper into the woods and keep running."

Since he didn't have an alternate plan, he said, "On three."

She tucked her weapon into her waistband and grabbed his hand. "Now."

Together they made a run for the denser forest, a yawning blackness that waited to swallow them whole.

But out of that darkness came a dozen flashlights, their beams blindingly bright as their pursuers encircled them.

Ian skidded to a halt, his arm snaking around Simone and drawing her tight against his side in a protective gesture. Bracing himself for the bullets he knew were going to come, he looked down into her face. "I'm so sorry."

She turned in his arms so that they faced one another. There was a soft click as she removed the magazine from her weapon. "No, I'm sorry."

The defeat in her voice made him want to cry. He heard a soft thud at their feet, but it was too dark at ground level to see what she was doing with her foot.

"This is my fault," she continued. "I failed, just as I did with Beth. I couldn't protect you, and now we're both going to pay the price. This is on me."

Obviously, something tragic had happened in her past for which she still carried a burden of guilt.

He should've listened to her and let Austin turn

around. She'd had a bad feeling, and he should have trusted her.

Resolved to not give up, he released her and held up his hands. "Please, let her go. She's not a part of this. She knows nothing."

"What are you doing?" she growled.

"Trying to save you," he told her. "You shouldn't have to die because of me."

"It's your lucky day, Delaney," a male voice with a heavy brogue called from the darkness. "The boss wants to talk to you and your girlfriend. Simone, is it?"

Fear mingled with a short burst of relief. At least they wouldn't die right here, right now. Ian didn't believe in luck, but he did believe in a loving God who answered prayers. Hopefully, Ian could convince the "boss" to let Simone go. There was still time to talk their way out of this. If there was one thing Ian had mastered from his father, it was the art of negotiation.

The men, some dressed in dark-colored tactical gear and others in mismatched camo, moved in, tightening the circle around them. The man who'd spoken before stepped closer. "Make no mistake. The boss may want to talk to you, but he'd be satisfied to see your corpse, as well. Don't make any sudden moves."

Rough hands separated them, pulling their arms behind their backs and tying them with ropes. Then they were pushed forward in the direction of the road, where they were forced into the back of one of the trucks. A young man climbed aboard and sat with his back against the tailgate. He held a high-powered rifle across his lap.

As soon as the truck began to roll forward, Ian let out a breath and leaned close to Simone, putting his forehead against her hair. Keeping his voice low, he said, "A momentary reprieve."

"Yes." She turned so her mouth was against his ear. "How do these men know my name?"

"I don't know." His eyes on their armed guard, he said into her ear, "Where's your weapon?"

"I buried it in the dirt as best I could. Best for them not to know I was armed. Or that I'm your bodyguard."

Ah, now he understood what she'd been doing and what the thud at their feet had been. Ian sent up a small prayer for God's provision. If they'd found her gun, they might have felt threatened enough to kill her. He realized this woman meant more to him than he'd thought possible. He had to see that she stayed alive. "If the opportunity presents itself, you escape."

She leaned away from him. The moonlight spilling across her face, creating shadows, but there was no mistaking the horror in her expression. "That's ludicrous. We have to have hope. There has to be a way out of this. Together."

Darting a glance at the thug with the gun, he said, "We have to put our hope in God above."

She relaxed next to him, settling her head on his shoulder. "Yes. Dear Lord, deliver us from these men. Save us from the criminals who want to do us harm. Be with us and make us strong in the face of our adversaries." Her soft voice floated through the air and wrapped around Ian like a comforting quilt.

He sent up his own plea. "Please, Lord, please hear our prayers. Amen."

Despite the circumstances, an unexplainable peace descended on Ian and he took comfort in the sharing of faith with Simone.

* * *

Simone kept her gaze on the passing scenery, hoping to identify any landmarks. "Do you recognize where we are?" she whispered.

"Not really," he said. "But judging by the position of the stars, we should be near town."

Good news. Leaning in close, she whispered, "Here's what we can do. Scoot so that we can reach each other's hands. We untie the ropes and jump out."

He made a noise in his throat that she took as agreement. They shifted slightly until they found each other's ropes. Almost immediately, her stomach sank as she realized they were dealing with constrictor knots, which were nearly impossible to untie. But they had to try. She hissed as one of her fingernails broke at the quick.

"You okay?" Ian's concerned voice came at her through the dark.

"Fine." She slanted their guard a peek. The young kid's head bobbed forward. Apparently, he wasn't too concerned that they would escape. "Just keep working at the rope."

"I can't make any traction with it. This is unlike any knot I've ever encountered."

"We have to keep trying." She hated how desperate her voice sounded.

The truck turned off the asphalt onto a winding dirt road.

"We're on the backside of the big mountain," Ian told her. "How can my father have something to do with this?"

The hurt in his tone pulled at her. "We don't know that he does."

But she had a sinking feeling they were being taken to the place where the encoded longitude and latitude intersected. In the morning, Deputy Rawlings and the new deputy, Leslie, would head out to the location. Would they find Simone and Ian's dead bodies?

The trees and the foliage grew thicker the deeper they went into the forest, the road harder to traverse. The stars were obscured. Even the moonlight barely cast its glow through the canopy of big tree branches overhead.

Finally, they came to a stop. Unfortunately, neither Simone nor Ian had been able to release themselves from the ropes, much to Simone's frustration.

They were pulled out of the back of the truck and brought to the center of what appeared to be some sort of camp with tents blending into the landscape and men carrying guns everywhere.

"On your knees." A man pushed her and Ian down to the ground.

"Please let my girlfriend go," Ian pleaded with the man. "She has nothing to do with this."

Simone clenched her jaw to keep from protesting his words. The ridiculously chivalrous man just couldn't get it through his head that she was the one who should be sacrificing for him. But she would use the fact the men thought she was merely Ian's girlfriend and not a threat. Let them underestimate her. She'd use it to her advantage when the opportunity arose.

A tall, dark-haired, bearded man walked out of one of the tents. The men moved back, creating a path for the man to walk toward them.

This must be the boss. "What is it you want?" Ian asked. "Money? I can get you money. Just release my girlfriend."

The man laughed. "I have to say it's very nice to see Ian Delaney begging."

NINE

Ian bit the inside of his lip until he tasted blood. They were on the backside of the mountain in some sort of militia camp. Lanterns hung from tree limbs, creating small pools of light and menacing shadows that prevented Ian from forming a clear lay of the land. Men of varying ages with guns circled them. Some had straggly hair and well-worn clothes, while a handful of others were definitely seasoned soldiers in black tactical gear. The ragtag mix confused and concerned him. What was this place?

Had he been looking for this camp when he'd set out in the helicopter?

Kneeling on the ground next to Simone in front these men, it took all the self-control Ian possessed to keep from saying something that might get him or Simone killed. Who was this guy mocking him? And why did he seem to know Ian?

Studying the man, Ian admitted something seemed vaguely familiar about him. He wasn't an employee of Delaney Holdings. Ian always made it a point to meet every employee, even those working abroad.

Their paths must have crossed somewhere else. And judging from the way his green eyes glittered with hostility, the meeting hadn't been a friendly one. Had it occurred during the time of his missing memories? Frustration burned in his gut.

What did this man want? Ian needed to figure out the best way to negotiate his and Simone's release. Or, at least, Simone's release. Though he doubted she would leave without him.

"I was told you'd lost your memory," the man said, shaking his head. "I'm not buying it."

"I have no memory of the last week," Ian insisted. Why would this man think he would lie? "I don't know you. There's no reason for you to hold us. I'm not a threat to you." He glanced at Simone and amended his statement. "*We're* not a threat to you."

The man sneered. "Of course you are. I can't take the chance you'll suddenly remember."

"Remember what?" Ian couldn't keep irritation from coloring his voice. "How do you know me? This is insane."

"Ian."

Simone's whispered warning had him reining his emotions. He tried for calm but wasn't sure he accomplished it. "My memory may never come back. I was in a helicopter crash, after all." The man smirked. Because he'd caused the crash that had brought down Ian's helicopter? "We don't know what you're doing here. You can move your base of operation and disappear. No one will be able to find you."

"We'll be moving soon enough. We haven't reached our goal yet."

"What is your goal?" Simone asked.

The man's sharp gaze focused on her. "Who's asking?"

Simone shrank away from the man. Ian frowned. What was she doing?

"I'm no one," she said, her voice small and low.

She didn't sound like the forceful, determined bodyguard he knew. Why was she acting so scared?

"Then don't worry your pretty little head about it." The man dismissed her with a roll of his eyes.

Ian winced, watching Simone carefully and praying she wouldn't react.

Though her jaw firmed for a split second, revealing to Ian her core of steel, her expression crumpled. "Please, sir, I don't know what's going on here. I barely know this man. We've only recently met. I'm not involved in any of this. Please let me go."

Understanding dawned for Ian. Smart of her to try to play on this man's sympathies. No doubt she wanted everyone to underestimate her so they wouldn't know exactly how much of a threat she would be once they undid the ropes keeping her hands behind her back. Admiration for the beautiful woman had Ian suppressing a smile.

The man gave a snort. "Well, isn't that just too bad. You should never have gotten mixed up with the likes of him."

Ian met his glare and was taken aback by the hatred.

The man spat on the ground. "The Delaneys are no good. They go back on their word. All of them."

Ian's gut twisted. This sounded personal. What had he done to this man? Or rather, what had his family done to this man? "What do you mean by that?"

His lip curled. "Ask your father about the Dresdens. Ask him to tell you what he did to them."

Ian's heart sank. This did have something to do with his father and the missing Dresden Group files. "My father's in the hospital. He's very ill. I was on my way to see him when your men kidnapped us."

"I know all about your father," the man said, his voice filled with derision. "Nurse Janice is keeping us apprised of the situation."

Cold dread stole Ian's breath. His fingers fisted behind him, the bindings at his wrists cutting into his flesh. "Why would she do that?"

"Because she's smart." He shrugged. "If she doesn't cooperate with us, we'll kill her son. It's that simple."

Anger had Ian stretching taut the ropes holding him captive. There had to be some way he could get them out of this situation, no matter how hopeless it seemed. For now, he and Simone were at this man's mercy. And, apparently, so were others in the Bristle community. "Who are you? Why are you doing this?"

"I'm the person holding your life in his hands. That's all you need to know."

"You're part of the Dresden Group," Ian stated. "What is it?"

A ghost of a smile flitted across the man's face. "Yes. Now enough of this chatter." He motioned to his men. "Tuck them away. I don't want to see them again until morning. I'm tired, and I need to think." He turned on his heels and stomped back to the tent from which he had emerged earlier.

Another man stepped forward. This guy wore jeans and a flak vest beneath a shearling coat. "You heard the boss. Get them up. Tie them to that tree." He pointed to a large pine on the other side of the wooden picnic table.

Two soldiers hustled forward, pulling Ian and Simone to their feet and pushing them toward the tree. They were forced to sit side by side on the cold, damp, pine-needle-covered ground, their backs to the tree. Ropes were fastened around them, securing their bodies to the trunk. The pressure from the rope across his chest bit into Ian's ribs, and his heart hurt with despair. How were they going to escape this place?

From his position, Ian had a clear view of the night sky through a break in the tree's limbs. He twisted his head to keep his eye on the men, making sure they didn't hurt Simone. She remained quiet, watchful and compliant, obviously keeping up the facade of his nonthreatening girlfriend.

The man who had galvanized the others into action walked over and squatted before them. His brown eyes were sympathetic as he secured additional ties around their ankles. "Don't do anything foolish," he said in a low voice. "They will kill you, and I doubt you want to die tonight."

"No, we don't," Simone murmured.

His gaze raked over her before he glanced at the two soldiers standing nearby with their automatic rifles. "Grab them some blankets. It's cold out here." One of the men nodded and jogged away.

"Why is this happening to us?" Simone asked the man. "What is this place? And who are you people?"

The man glanced over his shoulder at the soldier still standing watch. "I can't tell you that. But it will be best for you both if you just do as you're told."

The other guard returned with two blankets. The man rose from his squat and took the items, draping one over each of them. Then he met Ian's gaze. "Hang tight." He turned and walked away, leaving the two soldiers standing guard behind.

For a long moment, Ian and Simone sat in silence, letting the sounds of the night settle around them. The scent of pine mingled with the moss growing on the trunk of the tree and the dirt beneath them, clogging Ian's senses. He was glad he'd grabbed a parka on the way out of the house because the air was growing colder. "Simone, you doing okay?"

Beside him, Simone shifted against the rough bark of the tree, her eyes meeting his in the moonlight. "We're not dead. I'd say we're okay."

They weren't dead. Yet. He sent up a praise to God above.

Apparently growing bored of sentry duty, the two guards moved to sit at the picnic table. One of them lit a cigarette, the smell drifting toward Ian and Simone on the evening breeze.

Thankful the two men had given them some privacy, Ian lowered his voice to ask, "What do you think he meant by 'hang tight'?"

"I don't know," Simone answered in a soft whisper. "It was odd."

"What is my father mixed up in?" Patrick had done some erratic and eccentric things over the years, the most recent the treasure hunt that had caused so many problems for the town of Bristle Township, but his father was an honorable man. He would never involve himself in criminal activities. And there was no doubt in Ian's mind that these men were criminals. He wouldn't believe his father was knowingly in league with whatever was going on here.

"Obviously," Simone said, her voice soft, "this Dresden Group you stumbled onto when you were working was the catalyst for all of this."

"Right, but I still don't know what I'd discovered.

And since they wiped it from our servers, no one else will, either."

"Your father knows."

Anxiety tightened the muscles in Ian's neck and shoulders. "If they have Nurse Janice in their pocket, she could do something to keep him from saying anything. Do you think she'd hurt him?" He closed his eyes against the thought of harm coming to his father. The ache to do something, to fix the situation, made his blood hot. He hated this helplessness stealing over him.

"Honestly, I don't know." Simone's voice held a note of uncertainty. "I would think if they wanted him dead, it would've happened already. Plus, Mike is there."

His heart contracted. "That doesn't make me feel any better. Dad's still vulnerable to them. And Mike didn't answer your calls. What if they took him out?"

"I'll admit that worries me," she said. "But I met Nurse Janice. I have to believe she's only reporting back to them."

"But you don't know that. She's the one who called me. Insisted I come, alone, to see my father." Anger laced each word and tasted bitter on his tongue. "She drew me out of the house so they could kidnap me."

"Because her son is in jeopardy."

"Exactly. And so is my father." Frustration made his head pound. "This is so maddening."

"There's nothing we can do about it at this moment except pray."

He appreciated her calm presence even if he couldn't achieve the same state. "Good idea." Turning his troubles over to God had always brought him peace in the past. "Lord, we ask for your help in this situation. You are a

God of miracles, and we need a miracle. Provide us with an escape. Please protect my family. Protect us. Amen."

"Amen." After a moment of silence, she said, "There's something about that last guy."

"I was thinking the same thing," Ian said. "But I can't quite put my finger on what."

"His accent is different. South Boston," she said. "All the others I've heard talk have thick brogues."

"You're right. If I didn't know better, I'd think we were in Ireland." And that was very odd. Until tonight, he had yet to meet anyone from his home country in Bristle Township. What did it mean that so many armed Irishmen were gathered in the forest?

"I counted fifteen men so far," Simone said. "They're heavily armed—AK-47s and high-end handguns. But not all the men are equal. I think this is some sort of training camp."

A sick feeling tumbled through Ian's stomach. "Maybe the rumors *are* true."

"Rumors?"

He didn't even want to voice the whispered suspicions he'd heard over the past year. "There are some who say the Troubles in Ireland are going to start again."

"The 'Troubles'?" She stared at him, her gaze wide in the moonlight. "As in IRA?"

"It's just rumors." He prayed they weren't true. Too many had suffered because of the unrest in Ireland over the years. He couldn't imagine how many more would suffer if the unrest in his home country grew to the point of all-out war again. "But there's no way I believe my father could be involved in any of it."

"He had written down the coordinates of this militia camp."

There was no denying that fact. Ian's heart rate sped up. "But if the Troubles start up again, it would be bad for our company. We do a lot of importing and exporting out of Ireland and the UK."

"Maybe that's the reason behind what's happening," she stated. "The Dresden Group must be using your company to smuggle arms and men in and out of Ireland."

Ian groaned. Unfettered anger charged through him at the thought of his company being involved in illegal activities. Why would his father put his life's work at risk? "That could be what I discovered."

"You probably uncovered some discrepancy that led you to want to verify your findings."

"But why didn't I go straight to the authorities?" Even as the words left his mouth, the truth slammed into him. He would have wanted proof before sounding an alarm. Why? Because he hadn't wanted to appear foolish if he'd been wrong.

"Only you know the answer to that question."

What had his brother said to him? *Don't let your ego get the better of you*. He groaned. "My ego."

She flashed him a grin. "You don't say. Hmm."

He deserved her ribbing. "No need to rub it in."

She sobered. "But it does us no good to know what they are doing here unless we can escape."

"I've never felt so powerless in my life." Ian pulled at the restraints, chafing his skin against the ropes.

"We're not helpless. We have God on our side," Simone insisted.

"True." Ian settled back, forcing himself to find the same calmness Simone exuded. "Now who's looking at the glass half full?"

"Maybe you're rubbing off on me."

That elicited a soft laugh.

"Besides," she continued, "it's not over until it's over."

"Funny." He tilted his head back and stared at the night sky. Hopefully, it being over wouldn't equal their deaths.

Simone didn't think the situation was funny at all, but the last thing she needed was Ian giving up hope. So far, her defenseless-female act hadn't garnered the deferential treatment she'd hoped for. But she would keep it up as long as she could. She was certain the boss man wouldn't hesitate to do away with her if she gave him a reason.

"On a clear night, when the moon is full, you realize how big the universe is, so vast with so much we still haven't learned." Ian's words held a note of awe that she hadn't heard from him before. "And the stars, the glorious stars, twinkling like diamonds on black velvet."

She slanted him a glance at the poetic verse coming from his mouth. Who talked like that? Apparently wealthy men who were used to seeing loose diamonds on fabric. They came from such different worlds.

Speaking low enough that the guards wouldn't hear, she said, "The only loose diamonds I've ever seen were during a bust after a jewelry heist when I was on patrol with the Detroit PD."

"You deserve diamonds," he murmured.

What? She tucked in her chin and stared at his profile. The glow from the nearly full moon created shadows along the angular planes of his face. There was no denying that he was handsome. The stitches over his eyebrow only intensified his attractiveness in a way she didn't understand. But it was more than good looks that she found appealing about Ian.

"There's the Little Dipper. Do you see it?"

She looked at the sky but, to her, there was no rhyme or reason to the smattering of twinkling lights. She made a noncommittal noise in her throat.

Ian turned his gaze on her. "You don't like stars?"

She shrugged. "I've nothing against stars. I'm just not used to…" She sought the right word. Appreciating them wasn't right. *Noticing* was closer.

"Marveling at them?" he offered.

"Yes. Marveling." How did he do that? He seemed to understand her in unnerving and exhilarating ways.

Simone didn't want to be emotionally drawn in by this man. But she was. He wasn't what she'd expected when she'd taken this assignment. She'd expected to find the CEO of Delaney Holdings to be arrogant, to hide behind his wealth and to cower in the face of danger. Instead, Ian was confident but not self-important. He was also generous and brave. And it left her unsettled and more committed than ever to protect him. Something so far she had been failing at.

But first she had to create an opportunity for their escape.

She eyed the two guards at the picnic table. Both were now hunched forward, their heads on their arms. What would it take to convince them to untie her?

"What are you thinking?"

Ian's softly asked question snapped her attention to him. "We need these ropes undone."

"What do you suggest?"

"We get them to untie us." Easier said than done. But she still had to try.

"How?"

Good question. "Hopefully play on their sympathies."

Ian snorted. "Do you think they have any?"

"I'm praying so. Only one way to find out." Taking a breath, she slowly let it out to calm her racing heart.

"Hey!"

Neither of the men stirred.

Frustration had her gritting her teeth. She didn't want to alert the whole camp, even though there didn't appear to be anyone else wandering around. There had to be a way to get those two men's attention.

"Dude!" she said with a little more force.

The younger of the two guards popped up, his head swiveling.

"Hey!" she said again, softer.

The man spun around on the bench, a deep scowl on his face. He pushed himself to his feet and stomped over to them. "What?"

Exaggerating a demure countenance, she said in her best coaxing tone, "Please, I need to use the facilities."

He stared at her for a minute with clear indecision then shook his head. "I don't have permission to release you. You'll have to talk to Marcus or Joe."

"Then go get one of them," Ian said. "My girlfriend is suffering."

Simone arranged her face in what she hoped was a pained expression. Would the guy find some sympathy?

"I'm not disturbing them." The unease in his voice was clear. He walked away and resumed his seat at the table.

"Well, we know more than we did before," she said softly to Ian. "There's a Marcus and a Joe. And this kid is scared of them. Do either of those names ring a bell?"

Ian shook his head. "Common enough names."

Unfortunately, that was true. "I suggest we get some rest. We need to be ready in the morning when they come for us."

"In case I don't have a chance to tell you…" Ian's voice wrapped around her. "You are one brave and special woman. And I appreciate all you've done for me. I'm sorry I got you into this mess."

Surprise washed over her. He thought he was responsible. She knew just where the blame lay. On her shoulders. "This is on me. But I promise you, Ian, I'll do everything I can to make sure you live."

"I know you will," he said. "I have faith in you."

His words were meant to soothe but served to remind her that she had no control over this situation. Neither of them did. She leaned her head against his shoulder. "You humble me."

For a long time, they remained silent. The night sounds lulled her senses. The cold seeped beneath the blanket, making her shiver.

"Tell me about Beth."

She gasped in a shocked breath, coming fully awake. She hadn't meant to utter Beth's name and had hoped that Ian had forgotten. But in that moment before they'd been captured, there in the meadow when she'd thought for sure they were going to be mowed down by gunfire, she had revealed something she hadn't told anyone but her parents. Unburdening herself to Ian would be irresponsible, not to mention gut-wrenching.

What would he think of her if he knew she'd been the cause of someone's death? Someone she had sworn to protect?

Just as she had sworn to protect him.

TEN

"Look, we're going to get out of this," Simone said, hoping to put off Ian's question about Beth. "We don't really need to delve into my past."

"But I want to know." His voice took on a commanding quality that no doubt served him well in the boardroom.

She could feel Ian's gaze on her profile. She kept her eyes on the sky, though she didn't really see the stars through the burning tears pricking her eyelids.

"I want to know you, Simone. This person was very important to you. You said you failed her. How?"

If her hands hadn't been tied behind her back, she would have buried her face in them. Instead, she blinked back the tears, deciding her emotions were raw because of the situation. Not because it had been so long since anybody had taken a deeper interest in her beyond the superficial. She wasn't sure she trusted that Ian's curiosity wasn't some morbid need to know her dirty secrets. She shook her head. "I'm sorry I said anything. I shouldn't have."

"You thought we were going to die in that meadow. So did I," he confessed. "But we didn't."

"Thankfully."

"This Beth is important. Important enough for you to mention her when you thought it was the end."

"Why do you want to know?"

"Because if we *are* going to eventually die here, I want it to be with us knowing each other. You can ask me anything. I'm an open book to you, Simone."

She closed her eyes against the need to talk welling up inside her. She'd held in her angst and sorrow for so long. Even James didn't know the extent of her grief. He knew about the incident, of course, and he'd absolved her of any wrongdoing. So had the police department. But she hadn't absolved herself. She'd been responsible. Full stop.

"Beth was a childhood friend. Her family lived next door to mine. But when we got to high school, her father lost his job and they had to move. We didn't see each other for a long time." She bit the inside of her lip. "I should've stayed in touch with her. It never dawned on me that her life had become so hard."

"You were a teenager," Ian said. "Teenagers have a tough time thinking beyond themselves. That's what makes them so difficult."

She slanted him a glance. "How do you know this? You don't have any teenagers in your life, do you?"

"I once was a teenager," he said softly.

She made a face at him. "You know what I mean."

"I, actually, work closely with a teen shelter in Boston."

She stared at him. "Aren't you full of surprises. What do you do for this teen shelter?"

"The Delaney Foundation gives money," Ian said.

That did not surprise her. Ian Delaney didn't come across as the stingy type. "Doing good with your resources. I like that."

"But I also mentor several teenagers."

Unexpected and interesting. "Mentor? How so?"

"Many of the teens that come into the shelter are from broken homes," he said quietly. "I know what it is to lose a parent. Even though my mother died of disease, our family was forever impacted by the loss. Sometimes these teens just need somebody to guide them through their grief and anger. Help them discover their potential. We started a learning center where the teens can finish their GEDs and do college prep work."

Impressed and awed, she realized this man had more layers to him than she'd imagined. And her feelings for him deepened the more she learned. "I don't think it's a stretch to guess you've probably sponsored some college students." That seemed like something he would do.

"Yes, I have." He dipped his chin and eyed her. "I'm not going to let you distract me from my query, though. You lost track of Beth during your teen years. Then what happened?"

Her stomach twisted. She was hoping that deflecting the conversation would keep her from having to spill her guts. She could refuse. Was tempted to. But, for some reason she didn't understand, telling him suddenly seemed like the right choice. She might regret doing so, but now that she'd made the decision, she would follow through.

"I was a year into my job on patrol when I spotted Beth in the park. She'd gone down the dark road of drugs and all that entails."

"That's rough. I'm sorry."

She could still remember the shock of seeing her once vibrant friend looking gaunt, strung out. "Beth gave me a tip about a man she'd gotten involved with. He was abusive and a meth dealer. She also gave us the location of his lab."

"It was brave of her to tell you."

"Yes." Heaviness weighed down her shoulders. "I told her I could keep her safe. But my superiors wanted me in on the bust. I had to leave her in a motel, certain there was no way anybody would know where to find her."

"But I take it something happened."

"When we raided the warehouse, we got the goods and most of his crew, but we didn't get him." The burn of frustration and anger lit her belly, chased quickly by the guilt that always taunted her.

"By the time I got back to the motel, she was gone. We found her in a ditch three days later, her body battered and bruised. He'd gotten to her. He'd killed her."

"I'm so sorry."

The sympathy in his voice ate at her. "It was my fault. I shouldn't have left her."

"But your bosses wanted you at the bust. How could you've known what would happen?"

"I should have stood up to them."

"And risk your job? You had no way of knowing. You did what you had to."

"I should've at least arranged for more protection. For patrol to swing by and check on the motel."

"Do you think that would've helped? Seriously?"

"I don't know." Simone released a noisy breath. She'd gone around in circles in her mind over the choices she'd made that night and always ended up back in the same spot. "But I do know I didn't deserve a commendation."

"Did you ever find him?"

Her gaze dropped from the twinkling stars to the dark forest. Shame and guilt washed over her. "Four years later. I worked my tail off to get into Homicide, just so I could work her case. So that I could bring her murderer to justice."

"You're very tenacious."

She gave him a sharp glance.

He smiled. "A good trait. And I would guess you brought him to justice."

"Yes. I tracked him to the top floor of an apartment building. He made a run for it and climbed down the fire escape. It broke and left him hanging on the side of the building." She shook her head. "He was a monster with no conscience."

"What did you do?"

"It's what I didn't do. Or, at least, what I didn't want to do."

"You rescued him." The certainty in his voice grated on her nerves.

"Yes," she thundered. "Him dying wasn't going to bring Beth back. Me killing him would have ruined my life. So, yeah, I rescued him. I grabbed hold of him, and other officers came to help. He confessed to Beth's murder. Even laughed about it. He's serving a life sentence."

"Did he tell you how he found her?"

She was silent for a long moment then the admission tore from her. "Apparently, she called him to warn him and beg his forgiveness. He thanked her by killing her."

"Not to be harsh, but she brought it on herself. If she hadn't contacted him…" Ian said.

"That's what everyone tells me. But I trusted her, despite knowing what a mess she'd made of her life. Her death is on me."

"You gave her the benefit of the doubt, Simone," Ian

said. "Sometimes that's all you can do with people. They have to make their own choices, make their own way in life. And as frustrating as it is to watch them crash and burn, you have to do it. You have to let them reap or suffer from the consequences of their decisions."

His words dug into the guilt she carried. "If I'd done things differently, she wouldn't be dead. Nothing can change that."

"You don't know that he wouldn't have escaped without her calling him. You don't know that he wouldn't have killed her another time. You said he was abusive," he said. "And it does no one any good for you to carry around the burden of guilt for this woman's death."

Exhausted by both the conversation and the stress of their situation, she leaned her head back against the rough bark of the tree. "Go to sleep, Ian. We'll need our strength in the morning."

After a heartbeat of silence, he said softly, "For what it's worth, I'm proud of you."

It was worth a lot, but there was no way she could ever let him know. She closed her eyes, but sleep did not come. Every noise brought her senses alert. Would the boss of this bizarre gang go back on his word and kill them in their sleep? The possibility kept her on edge. But nobody came for them the rest of the night. The guards watching over them had fallen asleep at the picnic table.

Ian's head eventually dipped so that his chin rested against his chest. Sympathy went through her. He was going to have a kink in his neck in the morning. But better to feel the pain of muscles contracted in an unnatural position than to be dead with a bullet in the head.

* * *

The sun rose in shades of pink and orange, flickering through the late fall leaves. It'd been a very long time since Simone had watched a sunrise. The bloom of color, the burst of a new day, brought hope that somehow, some way, they would get out of the situation.

Wanting to make sure they were both alert and ready when the time came, she nudged Ian with her shoulder.

He groaned and rolled his neck. He turned his sleep-laden eyes on her. "Did you get any rest?"

"Enough. When they come for us, continue to play up that I'm the helpless girlfriend so they don't feel threatened by me. You just be the tough guy I know you can be."

He snorted. "I'm not a tough guy."

"Right. You're controlling, overconfident, stubborn..."

"Hey, now!"

"Teasing," she said with a smile. "You're actually nothing like I thought you would be when I took this assignment."

"Glad to hear that. I'm pretty sure you didn't like me when we first met in the hospital."

"It wasn't that I didn't like you..." she said.

"I know. It's probably more that you've protected men like me, men who expect everyone to jump at their command."

She deserved those thrown-back words. "Sorry about that. I did make assumptions based on previous experiences. Many of those whose lives I've protected would've been in puddles right now, sobbing into their knees."

"Believe me, if I thought it would help, I would do it."

"But it won't. And I appreciate that you're not."

"What are you planning?"

"Why do you think I'm planning something?"

"Because you're a smart lady, and you're always strategizing."

His assessment of her brought heat to her cheeks. "Okay, so you're right. Brace yourself."

"Now you have me worried." He grimaced. "I'll follow your lead."

Surprised and grateful, she flashed him a grin. Then she took a deep breath and let out a wailing sound that startled the birds in the trees and sent them flying.

Ian flinched. "Okay, I wasn't expecting that."

The two guards sleeping at the picnic table jumped to their feet and ran over. The older of the two slid to a halt in front of them. "Why are you acting the maggot?"

"Say what?" Simone had no idea what the man was talking about.

"It's Irish slang. He wants to know why you're making such a fuss."

Keeping her eyes on the soldier, Simone said, "You have to let me go. I can't stay like this anymore. I want nothing to do with this. Please, let me go."

The man sneered at her with a cruelty that churned her stomach. He raised the butt of his gun, clearly intending to smash it into her face. She braced herself for the blow.

"No!" Ian yelled. "You don't need to do that. What would Marcus or Joe say?"

The guy hesitated.

"I'll keep her quiet," Ian added. "There's no reason to hurt her."

A commotion at the other end of the camp drew everyone's attention. Men flooded from their tents, blocking the view. The two soldiers turned and jogged away, leaving Simone and Ian secured to the tree.

"Well, that was a bust," Simone grumbled, relieved the guard hadn't delivered the blow.

"You almost got yourself hurt," Ian accused. "Don't do that again. If anything happened to you—" He looked away, but not before she saw the emotion in his eyes. He really cared.

A strange fluttering in her heart made her ache to take him into her arms. But the best she could do was say, "I'm sorry, Ian."

He met her gaze and her breath caught. The tender affection in his eyes had her leaning as close as the ropes binding her to the tree would allow. Then he jerked his head and looked away.

She followed his stare to the other end of the encampment. The sea of soldiers parted as a man led two beautiful, saddled horses into the center of the camp. A mounted patrol jacket tied to one of the saddlebags caught her eye. Her stomach sank. "This isn't good."

"No, this isn't good. Where are the deputies?"

Simone prayed they weren't dead.

Ian's heart hurt. The horses without their riders was an ominous sign. Where were Deputy Rawlings and Leslie Quinn? They had been sent to investigate the area, and there had been no way for Ian and Simone to warn them of the danger they'd be facing.

He'd brought this to light. If only he could remember what he'd learned of the Dresden Group, none of this would be happening. If he'd just gone straight to the authorities and let them handle the situation rather than having to prove to himself that he was right, then no one would be in jeopardy.

"Marcus," the man without the Irish brogue yelled.

The boss, Marcus, stepped out of his tent. He and his second in command, presumably the man named Joe, conferred. Ian wished he could hear the conversation, but they were too far away and talking in low voices.

A few minutes later, two men led Rawlings and Quinn into the camp. A wave of relief to see the two alive swept over Ian. He recognized the tall blonde from around town. Both were dressed as civilians.

"I found these two snooping around the woods," one of the soldiers said.

"Well now, if it isn't Deputy Daniel Rawlings." Marcus turned to Leslie. "And who might this lovely lass be?"

"She's a friend," Daniel said. "We were out for a morning ride."

"Oh, come now, Deputy, you don't really expect me to believe that," Marcus said.

"What is the meaning of this? Who are you?" Daniel demanded. "You have no right to keep us here. And how do you know who I am?"

"I make it my business to know all the local law enforcement," Marcus said.

Ian willed Daniel to settle down. "How does Marcus know Daniel's a deputy?" he whispered to Simone.

"He may have more than Nurse Janice spying on the town," Simone answered.

"What should we do with them, boss?" the man holding Leslie by the biceps asked.

Marcus's gaze came to rest on Simone. "Take these two and the other woman out into the forest. We don't need them."

Ian's lungs seized. He couldn't let that happen. But how could he stop them?

"Steady," Simone said beneath her breath. "I need them to undo these ties."

"There's no way you can fight off fifteen men by yourself," Ian said. "Please don't tell me you would try it. You'd only get yourself killed."

She didn't respond, which made Ian more desperate to figure out a way to set her free. He tried again to loosen his ropes and only ended up chafing the skin on his wrist even more. Warmth flowed into his hands. He'd made himself bleed.

Joe stepped forward, his hands raised. "Boss, just a suggestion here, but we might want to hang on to all four of them as leverage. If this guy's a deputy, like you say, then more of them will be coming once they realize he's gone missing." Joe threw a glance at Ian and Simone. "I say we use these three as insurance to make sure Delaney cooperates."

Marcus stared at the man for a long moment. It seemed as if the whole camp held its collective breath.

"I don't think Marcus likes being challenged," Simone said subtly.

Ian braced himself, thinking that at any second the boss would shoot the man down.

But he just shrugged. "You're probably right, Joe. You have a good head on your shoulders. You haven't steered me wrong so far. Put the women to work in the mess tent. But keep a guard on them." Then he leveled a finger at Daniel. "Stash him somewhere. If he gives you any trouble, shoot him."

Marcus turned and strode toward his tent.

"What about Delaney?" Joe asked.

Marcus paused before speaking over his shoulder.

"Bring him to me." And then he disappeared inside the largest tent.

"This might be our chance," Simone said.

Ian was afraid she would do something that would get herself killed. "There has to be a way out of this for all of us. Joe's right. Once Daniel doesn't report back, Alex will come looking for him. And Nick will alert Alex once he realizes we're gone."

He could see she didn't like his logic. But it couldn't be helped. He would not let her sacrifice herself when there was no guarantee any of them would live.

"As much as it pains me to agree with you, you're right. We can't leave anyone behind. Though waiting to be rescued might not be an option." Each word vibrated with frustration.

The two men who had been guarding them earlier jogged over and released them from the tree but didn't undo their tied hands. They kept a tight hold on their biceps.

"If you've got to go to the jacks," one of them said, "this is your only chance."

Simone raised an eyebrow, her confusion clear.

"The facilities," Ian told her.

"Thank you," Simone said demurely.

The other soldier pointed at Ian. "You can go in the woods. But don't try anything. You heard the boss. He'd just as soon have you all dead."

Ian watched Simone being led away, his gut twisting with dread. He didn't want her out of his sight, but there wasn't anything he could do about it. He hoped she wouldn't do anything risky. There were too many armed men here for her to take on.

Ian silently prayed as he was marched out to the woods. *Please, Lord, provide us with an escape.*

ELEVEN

Simone fumed as the guard pushed her and Leslie into what they considered the mess tent. A larger tent than most of the others, save the one Marcus occupied, with several tables and benches arranged atop an earthen floor. A camp stove and food supplies sat off to the side.

"You heard the boss," the guard growled. "Make us some chow."

Simone faced the man. "How am I supposed to make anything with my hands tied behind my back?"

She needed him to free her hands. Then she'd be ready to act if an opportunity presented itself. The longer they stayed here, the more uneasy she grew. She didn't like this situation. There were too many variables at play.

He smirked. "Figure it out." He strode away and stood by the door. His malicious gaze bore into hers. His hands had a firm grip on the AK-47 strapped across his body.

"I've got it." Leslie picked up a serrated steak knife. "Turn around."

Simone presented her back. Leslie sawed through the ropes until they gave way. Relief and pain mingled as Simone rolled her shoulders, groaning as the muscles protested the prolonged position they'd been forced into.

She did a few stretches as she assessed the situation. Cutlery could be useful. Heavy pots and pans would make good weapons. The tent had only one opening, but that didn't mean there wasn't another way to escape the makeshift mess hall.

"Hey! Food. Now."

The guard's sharp tone sent a shaft of irritation slithering across Simone's flesh. Throwing a scathing glare over her shoulder, she tugged Leslie closer to the camp stove and turned her back on the man. Beneath her breath, she said to Leslie, "We need to get out of here."

"Agreed. But how?"

"You create a distraction to get our guard over here. Then I'll neutralize him."

Leslie slanted her a glance. "Neutralize?"

Simone made a face. "Render him unconscious. I'm not looking to kill him."

"Good to know. I understand you're ex–law enforcement."

"Shh." She picked up a can of baked beans and pretended to examine it. "They think I'm Ian's girlfriend."

Leslie cast a look at the guard then met Simone's gaze. "Right. Do what you need to, but if it comes to kill or be killed, don't hesitate."

Simone gave her a grim smile. "Don't worry. I won't. The same for you."

"We need to make a show of getting something put together here." Leslie grabbed a large bag of oatmeal. She pointed to the back of the tent where several gallon jugs had been stacked. "Let's get some water boiling."

Working together, they filled a large pot with water and set it on the camp stove to boil.

Remembering what Kaitlyn had said about Daniel

and Leslie having a history and questioning their ability to work together, Simone asked in a low voice, "What's with you and Daniel? I had the impression you two didn't get along."

Leslie snorted. "We grew up living next door to each other." She measured the oatmeal.

"Ah. Childhood rivals," Simone said.

"Something like that until it wasn't. Or, at least, so I'd thought. He took me to our senior prom then ditched me to go hang with his buddies. It was humiliating."

"Ouch."

Leslie shrugged. "Whatever. I'm over it. We're colleagues, nothing more."

Not sure she was buying Leslie's statement, Simone moved to the end of the table, pretending to search through the food supplies, waiting for Leslie to create the distraction that would afford her an opening to take the guard down. Suddenly a shot rang out from somewhere in the camp, jarring Simone to her core. Her eyes jumped to the man. "What happened?"

The guy smirked. "Probably your friends trying to escape."

Anguish flood her chest. Had they killed Ian? Or Daniel? Her heart cried out in protest. A prayer rose on her lips. "Please, no."

Leslie planted her forehead in her hand. "Oh, Daniel, what did you do?"

The torment in her tone tore at Simone. "Why do you think it's Daniel?"

Leslie lifted her head, her eyes filling with tears.

"Because he's a hothead. There's no way he'd comply with these guys." She wiped at her tears. "He's been the bane of my existence since I was a kid. If he got himself killed, I'll…" She spun away, her hands fisted at her sides.

Apparently, the woman's feelings ran deep despite her assertion that she was over him. Stepping closer, Simone put a hand on her arm. "Don't think that way. It could just as easily be Ian."

Simone's heart heaved at the thought of anything happening to him. Not only because he was her job but because she cared for him. Her heart had become involved. Something she'd never expected when she'd arrived in Colorado. And she couldn't find any regret in letting herself become emotionally involved with the man she was protecting. A sense of urgency raced along her limbs. She needed to find Ian. Now. "Let's hurry. The distraction?"

"Out of the way." Leslie moved so that she faced the pot of water and then purposely toppled it over with a yelp. Water poured into the dirt, steam rising.

The guard ran over. "What did you do? You clumsy—"

Simone came up behind the guard and slid her arm around his neck, cutting off his words. She braced his head with her other hand at the back of his neck so he couldn't squirm out of her grasp.

Leslie grabbed hold of the rifle strapped to his body and pried his fingers off the weapon. The man thrashed, trying to twist away from Simone, kicking at Leslie. But Simone held on until his body went limp and then she eased the unconscious man to the ground.

Leslie quickly undid the straps holding the rifle and hefted it in her hands.

Simone grabbed the SIG-Sauer from his hip holster. "Come on."

Before they could take a step, the flap to the tent flung

open and the second in command—the guy named Joe—
ran in. He skidded to a halt, his eyes wide.

Simone and Leslie both trained their weapons on him.

With his hands in the air, he said, "I'm on your side."

"Right," Leslie said. "You're just holding us captive,
that's all."

Another guard charged into the tent and aimed his
AK-47 at the two of them.

Simone's stomach clenched. Somebody was going to
die. She just prayed it wasn't going to be her or Leslie.
"Put down your weapon," she ordered.

The man with the rifle scowled. "No, you put your
weapons down."

Joe backed up a step. "I'd listen to them if I were you,"
he told the man.

"No way." The guard adjusted the rifle.

Leslie's finger moved to the trigger of the weapon in
her hand. Simone braced herself for gunfire.

Joe sighed. "Have it your way."

In a move that startled Simone, Joe swept the guard's
legs out from beneath him and, almost in the same move,
grabbed the man's hand and yanked it from the trigger
of the rifle strapped to him. He then delivered a blow to
the guy's larynx. The guard clutched at his throat. Joe relieved him of the weapon, turned the guy onto his stomach and glanced over his shoulder. "A little help here.
There are zip ties in my jacket pocket. There's duct tape
on one of those tables over there."

Blinking in disbelief, Simone exchanged a startled
glance with Leslie. Wary of this unexpected develop-
ment, Simone gave a nod. Leslie hustled to the table and
searched the supplies, returning with a roll of duct tape.
Simone found the zip ties in Joe's pocket. She quickly

bound the man's feet and his arms behind him. Leslie tore off a piece of duct tape and placed a strip across the guard's mouth.

"Do the same to that one," Joe said with a chin nod toward the man lying on the ground unconscious.

Simone and Leslie quickly bound and gagged the man.

Noise from behind them had Simone pivoting, the SIG coming up.

Leslie gave a small gasp as Daniel stepped through a hole he'd cut in the back of the tent. Shoving the automatic weapon into Simone's hand, she rushed across the tent floor. "What did you do?" She flung her arms around his neck. "You scared me."

The deputy's eyes widened and his mouth dropped open. Then he grinned. Grasping Leslie by the shoulders so that he could look into her face, he said, "Did you doubt for a second that I wouldn't get away and come looking for you?"

"What happened? Who fired their gun?" Simone asked.

Joe and Daniel exchanged a glance.

"Let's just say the guard and I had a disagreement," Daniel said.

"You could've gotten yourself killed," Leslie said.

He cupped her face. "Never. I needed to rescue my damsel in distress."

She slugged him, but the effort looked halfhearted. "What am I going to do about you?"

Daniel kissed her.

Simone was glad it turned out well for those two, but they weren't out of trouble yet. Any second now, more guards could come inside the mess tent and they'd all be dead.

"You've got to get out of here," Joe said.

Simone stared at him. "Who are you?"

"Joe Carlucci, ATF."

Realization dawned. "That's why you seemed familiar," Simone said. "I've worked with your brother, Anthony."

Joe smiled. "Yes, you have, Simone Walker. I recognized you the minute I saw you. You helped Anthony rescue his now wife when she was kidnapped."

"What are you doing here?"

"I was undercover. We needed to know what this militia was up to." His lips twisted in a wry scowl. "But now…" His gaze went to the still-conscious man currently staring daggers at him.

Simone groaned. "Sorry we blew your cover."

Joe shrugged. "It was bound to happen sooner or later. I didn't know Marcus was going to sabotage Delaney's helicopter until after the fact. If I'd known, I would've stopped it."

There was nothing to be done about the past. She was thankful Ian hadn't been killed. "Do you know what this is all about?" She made an encompassing gesture toward the camp.

"A training center for Irish militants," Joe said.

As Ian had suspected. "I mean…why are they targeting Ian Delaney?"

"Marcus has some kind of beef with the Delaney family. But he's keeping the details close to the vest. Though—"

Daniel and Leslie joined them, interrupting Joe. "So, what's the plan?" Daniel asked.

"You three need to get out of here and bring back the

cavalry. I'll do what I can to make sure Delaney stays safe," Joe said. "The horses are tied up east of the camp."

Simone shook her head. "I'm not leaving without Ian."

"There's no way to get to him," Joe told her. "Not without alerting the whole place."

"Then you'll have to distract the camp," she told him.

"As soon as somebody finds these two, I'm toast," Joe said. "I'll be leaving ASAP."

"Then we better make sure they don't find them," Daniel said.

"We can drag them outside and hide them in the woods," Leslie said.

Daniel grinned at her. "Good idea."

"I have them occasionally," Leslie quipped. There was no mistaking the tender affection in her eyes.

Their bantering reminded Simone of the way she and Ian were together when not dodging bullets. And it made her heart ache. She had to find a way to rescue him.

"Simone, grab his legs," Joe said, referring to the conscious guard.

Grasping the man by the ankles, she lifted while Joe got beneath his arms. They carried him, bucking and squirming, out the back of the tent. Leslie and Daniel transported the unconscious guard the same way. They took them about sixty feet from the camp and sat them on the ground, their backs up against a lodgepole pine. Using the duct tape, Joe bound them to the tree.

"Find branches and leaves and whatever we can use to cover them up. That will buy us some time."

Once they had the men camouflaged, Simone turned to Daniel and Leslie. "You two take your horses and go for help."

"What are you going to do?" Leslie asked.

"I'm going to find Ian and get him out of here."

"We should back you up," Daniel said.

Simone shook her head. "We need to split up. Do you still have that knife you used to cut the back of the tent?"

Daniel retrieved the hunting knife from his waistband. He held the handle out to Simone. "I don't like leaving you behind."

Leslie put her hand on Daniel's forearm. "The smarter play is for us to get help."

It was clear the man wanted to argue with her, but then he nodded. He looked at Simone and Joe, his expression grim. "Don't get yourselves killed before we return."

"We don't intend to," Simone retorted.

Daniel and Leslie hustled away.

Simone turned to Joe. "Do you think you can distract Marcus long enough for me to free Ian?"

"You know it."

"Then let's make a plan." If it was the last thing she did, Simone was going to make sure Ian got away before Marcus decided to kill him.

Ian's heart pumped in his chest as the echo of a gunshot lingered in the air. "What happened?" he demanded of Marcus.

Marcus shrugged. "Maybe one of your friends decided not to play nice."

Ian sent up a silent, fervent prayer. *Please, Lord, don't let Simone, Daniel or Leslie be dead.*

He tested the ties holding him to the chair as Marcus paced. At least his hands weren't strapped behind him in an awkward position any longer. "What is it you want?"

The man stopped pacing. "You seriously don't know who I am?"

"I don't," Ian said. "If we met sometime in the last week, then I've forgotten you."

"Let's try about twenty years ago."

Ian tucked in his chin. "Twenty years? I was at boarding school in Switzerland. You were there?" He did not remember this man being one of his classmates.

Marcus snorted. "Your mother's funeral."

Confusion and outrage twisted in Ian's chest. "You were at my mother's funeral?"

In the days leading up to his mother's death, Ian, Nick and his father had sat by his mother's side. She'd been fragile, weak but so brave. Her last words of love still resounded in his memory. By the day of the funeral, Ian had been blind with grief. The service and memorial afterward were a blur.

"Yes, I was there." Marcus moved to a makeshift dresser and picked up a small framed photo.

Curiosity itched at Ian. He couldn't see the image on the picture. "Why?"

Setting the frame facedown, Marcus resumed his pacing. "You'll have to ask your father. That is, if you live long enough to see him again."

Ian couldn't fathom why this man, who would've been fifteen, like Ian, at the time, would attend his mother's funeral. "What is the connection between our families?"

Marcus stopped, his fists clamped at his sides. "We're done talking about this. Joe was right. We have to move. As soon as the sheriff realizes the deputy and you are missing, men will come looking. This is all your fault. You shouldn't have gone snooping into things that were none of your business."

"This has to do with the Dresden Group files." Ian tried once again to recall what he'd been looking at that day. What in those files threatened Marcus and his operation? Ian thought about his conversation with Simone when they had been tied to the tree. He narrowed his eyes on Marcus. Dread crimped his chest. "Are you with the New IRA?"

Marcus swung his gaze to him. "There is no such thing."

"Yes, there is."

Over the years, there had been bombings and attacks perpetrated by the extremist group throughout England and Northern Ireland. Yes, there had been a truce called in the late nineties, but those dedicated to the cause had gone underground. And with the world economy the way it was going, Ian had no doubt the paramilitary group would take advantage and try to liberate Northern Ireland from British rule once again. "You're training men here to send back to Ireland and using my company to do it."

Marcus sneered. "Your company." He spat on the tent's dirt floor. "There's a lot your father hasn't told you."

Ian would have to deal with his fear and worry that his father was somehow involved with this militia later. Right now, he needed as much information as he could get. Because if he escaped this situation, he was going to make sure he didn't forget any of it. "Why don't you just tell me what's going on? It would save us both a lot of time."

Before Marcus could say another word, the tent flap flung open and Joe ran inside. "There's a problem at the mess tent. You better come."

Had something happened to Simone? Ian's stomach dropped. Joe met his gaze with a look that Ian didn't know how to interpret. "My girlfriend? Is she okay?"

Without answering, Joe turned back to Marcus. "Are you coming?"

Marcus barely spared Ian a glance as he rushed out of the tent with Joe.

Desperate fear had Ian pulling against the restraints with such force that the chair toppled over. He landed hard on his shoulder, the pain reverberating all the way to his teeth. A noise from behind raised the hairs at the base of his neck. Alarm twisted in his gut. He craned his neck, trying to see what was coming. The sound of pounding footsteps had him bracing for a blow.

And then Simone was there, kneeling at his side and using a knife to cut the ties binding him to the chair.

He scrambled to right himself and grabbed hold of her shoulders to make sure she was real. "You're okay? I thought something had happened to you. Joe said there was a problem in the mess tent."

"A distraction." She pulled Ian to his feet and held on to him as the blood rushed to his head. "We've got to go."

He cupped her face with his hands. "I thought I'd lost you." And the realization that he was well on his way to falling for this woman had his heart beating in his throat.

She nuzzled his shoulder for moment. "You're not getting rid of me that easily." Grabbing his hand, Simone tugged him toward the back of the tent. "Come on. We have to leave before Marcus realizes what's happening."

They slipped through the hole she had cut in the tent and ran into the forest away from the camp.

"We should go uphill toward the resort," he said.

"No, they will expect that." She shoved something into his hands. "We're going here. We have to give Daniel and Leslie time to bring back reinforcements."

He looked at what appeared to be a crude drawing of a map leading to a stick-drawn structure. "A cabin?"

"No, a hunter's lean-to. Joe said to head there."

"What's with this Joe character? You trust him?"

"He's undercover ATF," she said.

Dodging the branch of a tree, Ian asked, "How do you know for sure he's telling the truth?"

"His brother worked with us a few years back. That's why he seemed familiar."

They made their way deeper into the trees. The thick canopy overhead obscured the sun, leaving the forest in shadowed gloom. He was thankful it was early fall rather than winter and they didn't have to contend with snow.

The sound of men shouting echoed behind them. They were being pursued. Was the ATF agent still alive?

Simone pulled him against a tree. "They're close."

He nodded, his arms holding her tight as he listened.

"They're tracking us," she said.

Her grim tone had anxiety racing along his limbs. "What now?"

"Joe said there's a creek we have to cross. We need to get to it."

Pushing away from the tree, Ian gestured. "Lead the way."

He followed Simone through the forest, the branches tearing at his jacket. Exposed roots caught his feet, making him stumble in his haste. They broke through the tree line to a small creek with sandy shores.

"Perfect." Simone slipped off her shoes. "Take your shoes and socks off and roll up your pants."

Ian stared at her. "We're going to cross the water? Shouldn't we follow the creek to civilization?"

Rolling her pant legs to above her knees, she said,

"We need to get to the other side and then head to the lean-to. That's the plan."

He watched the water rushing over the rocky bottom. "It will be freezing."

She arched an eyebrow. "Are you questioning my judgment?"

There would've been a time not too long ago when he would have balked at her directive. But she'd proved to be trustworthy and competent. He had to trust she knew what she was doing.

Slipping off his shoes, he said, "Not today. Let's get out of here."

TWELVE

Ian hastily rolled his pant legs up past his knees and then held his socks and shoes above his head as he stepped into the icy stream. His breath seized in his lungs. Everything inside him urged him to back out of the water, but he forged ahead. Within moments, the lower halves of his legs were numb. He kept pace with Simone as she hurried downstream for several yards. His feet slipped on the slimy rocks. More than once, he thought he was going down, but he managed to stay upright.

"Here." Simone careened to the left, splashing through the water out onto the soft, sandy creek bank on the opposite side.

He'd never been so glad to feel the dry earth beneath his feet.

She pulled at his elbow. "Keep going."

Grimacing, Ian nodded. Not pausing to put their socks and shoes back on, she urged him into the forest. The prickle of pine needles and sharp rocks kept him in a perpetual grimace. He marveled that Simone showed no signs of discomfort. When they were a good fifty feet from the creek, she stopped, steadied her backside

against a tree, and put her socks and shoes back on.
"Hurry!"

Bracing his hip against the same tree, Ian brushed
off the debris clinging to the bottom of his feet and attempted to pull his socks on. The cotton-blend fabric
stuck to his wet skin, but he successfully yanked them
on. He managed to get his socked feet into his shoes just
as a chill raced up his body. Lowering his damp pant legs,
he wished for a warm fire and dry clothes. The midday
sun barely penetrated the shadows of the forest.

"Grab a branch or something to wipe away our footprints," Simone said.

She went to a fallen log and broke off a bushy twig.
Ian found a long, thin limb with shoots of foliage. Using
their makeshift brooms, they swept at their footprints as
they moved farther into the forest. Despite the cold of the
creek lingering on his feet and legs, Ian grew hot beneath
his jacket. But he knew if he took the coat off, his sweat
would cool and he would catch even more of a chill.

"You seem very comfortable in the outdoors. Is Running from Bad Guys in the Forest 101 a class they teach
in bodyguard school?" Ian asked as he brushed away
his footprints.

"Hardly. My parents loved to take us kids camping
during school breaks," she told him.

"How many kids are in your family?"

"I have two older brothers."

"Did you enjoy camping?"

Simone held up a finger, silencing him. She paused to
listen, he assumed to see if they were being pursued. He
waited, catching his breath. The only sounds he could
discern were those of the crickets and the rustle of the
wind in the pines.

Seemingly satisfied their pursuers weren't close, she said, "I did enjoy camping. Have you ever gone?"

"No. Today has been the closest I've come," he told her as they resumed sweeping away their path and continued deeper into the woods. He longed for a flashlight.

"Don't hold today's example against camping," she said. "I would imagine your family vacations were much more…extravagant."

"Before my mother's death, we took the yacht out. Those family outings were the best." The memories of the vessel cutting through the water, the wind whipping through his hair, and the sun on his face were some of his best from his childhood. "My father sold the boat after she died. From then on, family gatherings were on dry land and usually at the house or a resort."

"Do you miss being on the water?"

He gave the question some thought. "I do." The admission was a revelation. When this ordeal was over, he would look into purchasing a small boat for himself. And take Simone out on the water. "Have you been boating?"

She slanted him a glance as she ducked under a low-hanging branch. "I've been in a canoe and a kayak."

"Not the same."

"I would imagine not."

"I'd like to take you out on the ocean sometime," he said. He wanted to see her experience the thrill and freedom of zipping over the water's surface. The fact that he was thinking of a future with her in it caused him to misstep. He nearly took a face-plant into a tree, but she grabbed him by the arm, keeping him upright and safe.

"Careful," she said. "Are you dizzy? Do you have a headache?"

He'd like to blame the sudden rise in blood pressure

on the injuries he'd recently sustained, but he knew that wasn't it. His heart had picked up speed because he wanted to keep this woman in his life. For now. For always. Reeling from the realization, Ian rubbed a hand over his face. "I'm fine."

He moved away from her as he sorted out his feelings. He couldn't remember ever feeling this way about any woman. Was it the chaos and trauma of the situation making him think he was falling in love with Simone?

Up ahead, he saw what looked like a rickety structure made of rotted plywood and withered tree branches. Relieved to have a distraction, he said, "We've arrived."

Simone held up her hand, indicating for him to wait as she stepped into the lean-to. She returned a second later and waved him forward. "All clear."

Hanging on to the thin branch, he entered the small, gloomy, two-by-two structure. His nose twitched at the moldy odor permeating the space. Ian wasn't a hunter, so he didn't get the lure of waiting for game in something so dismal.

"You can leave the tree outside." Simone gestured to the limb he held. "You don't need it now."

"Not necessarily," he replied. "Since I'm unarmed, I need something to use in case we're ambushed. If I strip the shoots off, it could be a weapon." Plus, it'd give him something to do with his hands and keep his mind occupied from thoughts of the future. He didn't have a clue how she felt about him, and the last thing he wanted was to set himself up for heartache.

"Good idea. I have a knife." She produced Daniel's sheathed knife from inside her jacket pocket. "But first, eat." She tugged a granola bar from her other pocket and handed both to him.

"Where did this come from?" Setting both the limb and knife down, he ripped the wrapper off the bar and took a bite, savoring the burst of salty and sweet.

"The mess tent," she said, unwrapping her own bar. "I grabbed a couple before I took off."

"I never thought I'd appreciate nuts and raisins smashed together in rice syrup as much as I do right now," he said. "What I wouldn't give for some water."

"I didn't see any small bottles of water, but they had big gallon ones. How did they get all their supplies into the forest without anyone noticing?"

"If they were posing as hunters, no one would think twice about it." Ian finished the last bite of the bar, already feeling a bit better.

"True."

Taking a seat on the floor and stretching out his legs, he picked up the knife and began to strip the limb bare. "Are we going to just wait here to be found? By either the good guys or the bad guys?"

"Let's pray it's the good guys." Simone leaned against the doorway. "Joe told me something interesting right before he went into the tent to distract Marcus."

"Yeah, what?"

"Marcus isn't the boss."

Ian's heart thumped. "What?"

"He answers to someone named KC."

"KC? Like the letters? Or Casey, the name?"

She shrugged. "Beats me. But there's somebody else calling the shots."

"I don't know anyone who goes by either of those monikers." A heavy dread made him scowl. "But unfortunately, I'm sure my father will." He told her what Marcus had said about being at his mother's funeral and how Ian should ask his father for answers. "I wish I'd thought to grab that framed picture. That might have held answers."

"We just have to make sure we get out of here alive so we can learn what secrets your father's keeping," she said.

Ian watched Simone as she peered out of the opening of the lean-to. Her pants were plastered to her shapely calves. Her hair had unraveled from the bun she'd put it in when they'd left the house yesterday. Though it was dark inside the structure, the afternoon light spilled across her beautiful face. She was so determined and fierce, his heart ached.

He would gladly give up knowing any secrets to make sure this woman stayed alive. She'd come to mean more to him than he'd ever thought possible. He prayed there would be time once they were out of the woods, and safe, for him to examine and explore the growing feelings crowding his chest for this woman.

But he knew he would do anything, even give up his own life, for her. And that scared him almost as much as knowing that Marcus and his men wanted him dead.

Simone straightened. Tension radiated off her like a neon light. "Do you smell that?"

He sniffed the air. Alarm jolted through him as his senses processed the distinctive scent curling through the air. "Smoke." He scrambled to his feet and joined her at the opening to the lean-to.

A distant glow came from the direction of the camp and lit the night sky. The popping and crackling of trees going up in flames broke the quiet of the woods. A deep roar, as if the sound were rumbling up from the ground, shuddered through Ian. "The forest is on fire!"

"Change of plans," Simone said, a thread of panic lacing each word. "We have to head to the resort to warn them."

"And get out of the path of that fire." He tucked the hunting knife into his coat pocket and grabbed his now smooth stick. "Do you think the blaze was deliberate?"

"Your guess is as good as mine."

Together, they began the arduous trek uphill, fighting gravity and the thickening smoke as the blaze raced through the trees. He hoped someone had called the forestry service. Would the creek hold back the flames? Or would the blaze jump to the other side? Could they outrace the fire?

The night sky glowed orange as trees went up in flames and appeared like ghastly specters; the stuff of nightmares. The air burned Ian's lungs and stung his eyes. The taste of smoke made him gag. "We've got to cover our faces."

Immediately, Simone shrugged out of her jacket and her pantsuit coat. Then she attempted to rip off the sleeve of her button-down shirt.

"Here, let me," Ian said. Taking the hunting knife from its sheath, he cut the cotton fabric away from her arm.

"Cut the other sleeve, as well." She turned so he had access to that arm. "We'll tie them around our faces."

Once both sleeves were detached from her shirt, she put her suit coat and jacket back on. Ian handed her a sleeve, and she held it over her nose and mouth and tied it behind her head like a bandanna. Ian did the same. The cotton helped to filter the smoke, but there was nothing to be done about their eyes. He blinked through the stinging tears, trying to clear his vision.

They set off again. Heat from the conflagration chased

them uphill. Ian kept a litany of prayers going. He had no idea how close or how far they were from the top of the mountain. Animals scurried from beneath bushes. A fox streaked past them without hesitation. Birds took flight, their cries drowned by the inferno destroying the beautiful lodge pines and conifers, and everything that called the forest home.

Suddenly, Simone motioned him to halt. He stopped beside her and looked at her questioningly.

She spun, drawing her weapon.

Ian searched the hazy forest but couldn't see anyone. Visibility was only a few yards through the thick smoke. He silently raged with despair that he and Simone would die out here, trapped between a fire and Marcus's men. They needed to find shelter, cover, anything that would provide them a safe haven from the threats bearing down on them.

Simone couldn't shake the sensation they were being stalked as they raced to escape the fire. The need to move galvanized her into action. She jammed the gun back into her pocket, took Ian's hand and ran, pushing herself and him to the limit of their endurance. Her breath wheezed from her constricted chest. Ash rained down. Smoke pricked at her eyeballs like a thousand tiny needles.

They needed to reach the resort. They would be safe there. There had to be a way off this mountain. Surely by now the forestry department was battling the blaze, right?

As if in answer to her question, the whine of an engine reached her ears. She searched the sky.

"There!" Ian pointed to a large plane, barely visible above the treetops, coming toward them, flying low and dumping water in its wake. He waved his arms in an effort to gain the pilot's attention. Simone doubted they could be seen through the thick smoke, but soon they would be drenched from the release of water.

"Take cover!" she yelled, though she had no idea where to go. She couldn't see anything beyond where they stood except trees and foliage.

Ian pulled her forward until they ran smack into a large bush. He shoved her toward the ground. "Get underneath."

They wiggled under the thick bramble bush, the limbs sticking in her hair, ripping her jacket. A stinging on her cheek made her wince. No doubt she'd have a nice scratch.

Within seconds, a deluge of water drenched the area where they hid. Water dripped into the collar of Simone's jacket and sent a shiver of dread down her spine. Would they survive this fire?

They had to. She couldn't have Ian's death on her conscience. He needed to live. To stop what Marcus was doing, whatever it may be. To sail again. She wanted to introduce him to the joys of camping that she'd experienced growing up. She wanted to know if he felt the same developing connection she did.

She felt Ian leave their protective space, so she fought her way out of the brambles and shook off the spray that had made it through the thick foliage and soaked her clothes. Glancing around, she couldn't find Ian. "Ian?"

Panic burst in her chest. Where was he?

A noise close by alerted Simone a heartbeat before two men materialized out of the haze. Sooner than she could draw her weapon, one man rushed forward to snatch her, twisting her arm behind her back. He had on night vision goggles that no doubt could see through the oppressive smoke of the fire.

The other man stepped forward from the depths of the haze, also wearing the specialized goggles. "Where's Delaney?"

She recognized Marcus's voice, but he stood far enough away, she couldn't make out his features, only the black apparatus covering his face. Assessing her chances of escape, she contemplated taking down the man holding her, before Marcus—and others—put a bullet in her.

Thwack. Thwack.

The man holding Simone jerked, his hands falling to his sides as he crumpled to the ground. Simone searched for Ian as she stuck her hand in her pocket, her fingers curling around the weapon.

"Argh!" Marcus yelped as another *thwack* filled the air.

Simone rushed closer to where Ian was using the stripped-down tree limb like a fighting stick and thrashing Marcus.

"Drop the weapon," Ian growled at the man with a jab and another hit.

Marcus doubled over, letting the handgun he held fall to the ground. But he reached for a knife strapped to his leg and came up swinging, the blade slicing the air, aiming for Ian's throat.

"Watch out!" Simone shouted, terror slicing through her as the knife blade barely missed its mark.

The air filled with a rhythmic sound that reverberated inside Simone's skull.

She couldn't get a clean shot at Marcus. Ian was too close and moving too much as he used the long stick to smack the hand holding the knife, which he followed with a series of hits until Marcus went down again.

Roaring hot anger flooded Simone. She took the opportunity to pounce on Marcus. Wrestling the knife from his hand, she placed her knee in his back and the barrel of the SIG at the base of his neck. "Just give me a reason."

"Simone. Simone, honey, think about what you're doing."

Ian's gentle touch and soothing voice penetrated the fog of anger clouding her mind. She lifted her eyes, blinked through the stinging smoke, and met his soft gaze above the swath of cloth covering the lower half of his face. Then she spotted the others surrounding them. Her heart jolted when she noted the letters ATF emblazoned in bright yellow across the front of several flak vests. And the noise she'd heard registered as helicopters hovering in the air, black ropes dangling from the doors the agents had used to rappel to the ground.

With a wave of relief, she lifted her hands away from Marcus.

An agent stepped forward and took the gun from her hand. "Good job, Miss Walker." His voice was muffled by the N95 mask covering his mouth and nose.

"Joe! You're alive. Praise God." It was good to see the agent hale and hearty.

Ian reached out a hand to help her off Marcus and slid an arm around her waist.

Two agents then pulled the man to his feet and handcuffed his hands behind his back.

"Let's get you all out of here," Joe said.

"Wait." Ian detached from Simone and got in Marcus's face. "Who is Casey?"

Marcus sneered. "Lawyer."

Simone slipped her hand into Ian's. "We can sort this out later." For now they were safe. But somewhere out there was the person orchestrating the threat against Ian. And until that person was caught, she had a job to do. Though protecting Ian had become very personal.

Ian squeezed her hand and stepped back so the ATF agents could take Marcus and his cohort away.

Simone watched them walk into the hazy smoke then turned to Joe. "How did you find us? Who started the fire? Did Daniel and Leslie make it to town?"

"Whoa. I'll answer all your questions when we reach the sheriff's station," Joe said. He pointed to the sky where rescue baskets were being lowered from the helicopter. "Your ride awaits."

THIRTEEN

The big Chinook helicopter, piloted by the National Guard, landed like a feather on the helipad atop the Bristle Township Sheriff's Department building. Though Ian had paid for, and used, the platform after the structure had been decimated during the treasure hunt his father had initiated, he'd never been more grateful to have commissioned the helipad.

He helped Simone climb out of the big bird, the rotors beating the air around them. Joe and the other ATF agents hopped out, along with the two prisoners. They all hustled into the building, taking the stairs to the main area. Marcus and his thug were taken directly to interrogation rooms.

Alex clapped Ian on the back. "So glad to see you safe."

Appreciating the man's friendship, Ian said, "It's good to be here. But I wouldn't be if not for Simone." He looked over at her.

A soft smile graced her lips before she turned her attention to Alex. "Sheriff, do you know if my coworker Austin was found?"

"Yes, he was," Alex said. "He's at the hospital recovering from his injuries."

"That's good." A weight seemed to lift from Simone's shoulders.

Ian felt the same relief. He'd hated leaving the other Trent Associate bodyguard behind.

Daniel and Leslie joined them.

"We were worried you two wouldn't survive the fire," Leslie said, giving Simone a hug.

Simone turned to Joe. "How did the fire start?"

"Marcus," Joe said. "When he discovered that all of you had escaped, he went ballistic and overturned the table with the camp stove. The flame lit the supplies on fire and the tent caught the flames."

"Did he suspect you were involved in our escape?" Ian asked.

Joe shook his head. "No, those acting classes I took in high school must've paid off. He directed me to get everybody out of the camp and safely away. Then he and one of his men took off after you."

"What about the guards we tied to the tree?" Simone asked, worry darkening her expression.

"I got them to safety. But not before I called in reinforcements. The whole camp was rounded up and taken away by ATF."

"How did you find us?" Ian asked.

"The National Guard has infrared sensors on their helicopter," Joe told them. "Gotta love technology."

"We are thankful. How much damage has the fire done?" Simone asked.

"Several hundred acres," Alex reported. "But the forestry service has a fire line established and have contained ten percent so far. We're hopeful the fire will be one hundred percent controlled soon."

"What's going to happen to Marcus?" Leslie asked.

"He'll be taken into federal custody," Joe said.

"We need to know who is behind this." Ian couldn't keep the frustration from his voice or the acid from churning in his gut.

Joe shrugged. "Marcus has lawyered up. So have his men. But we will work on them. Eventually, they'll have to give up the leader."

"That's not encouraging," Ian said. "Until then, someone out there wants me dead."

Simone stepped closer to him. "They'll have to go through me."

"No doubt." He held her gaze. Ash smeared her face. Matted clumps of hair had escaped her messy bun, and dark circles rimmed her eyes. He thought her the most beautiful woman on earth.

"Do you think anyone besides Marcus knows who this Casey person is?" Simone asked, though her eyes never left Ian's.

"Hard to say," Joe answered. "I was undercover with the militia for five months. Marcus was the only one allowed to have contact with the outside world."

Tearing his attention from Simone, Ian said, "Let me in the room with him. I'll make him talk."

"That's not going to happen," Alex said. "As desperate as we are to know the identity of the mastermind targeting you, we must adhere to the law and the suspect's rights."

"What about Nurse Janice? Marcus bragged he had the nurse doing his bidding," Ian said. "My father is in danger."

"Then we better get over to the hospital," Alex said. "Daniel, you're in charge. Give Agent Carlucci whatever he needs. Ian, you'll ride with me. Leslie, if you could follow with Miss Walker?"

Simone sat in the front passenger seat of the sheriff's department SUV with Leslie at the wheel. Ahead of them, Ian rode with the sheriff. She didn't like not being with him but knew he'd be safe in Alex's care. It was probably good for them to have some space. The past twenty-four hours had been intense and emotional. Being kidnapped and escaping into the forest only to face a fire and armed men had a way of making a person reevaluate their priorities in life.

She didn't regret joining Trent Associates and protecting people. Providing security for those in trouble satisfied her. But at the end of each assignment, she went home to a lonely one-bedroom apartment. Sure, she had her family back in Detroit. She loved her parents and her brothers. But they had their own lives, full and happy ones. She had a job.

She wanted more.

She wanted connection and belonging.

She wanted to explore the growing feelings she had for Ian. But that couldn't happen until the threat to his life was eliminated.

Needing a distraction, Simone studied Leslie. The blonde wore the uniform of the sheriff's department. It was a good look for her. "So, you and Daniel. What a kiss."

A soft smile graced Leslie's face. "That was unexpected."

"But not unwanted?"

"True. Daniel and I had a long talk after we got back."

"You've forgiven him?"

"Yes. He'd apologized in the past, but I wasn't ready to hear it or to forgive him. But thinking he might be dead made me realize I was holding on to my hurt like a shield."

"Because you didn't want to be hurt again," Simone commented. "I get that."

"The weirdest thing is, he ditched me that night because he liked me too much. He was afraid that if we got together and actually started dating, it would derail my plans."

"Your plans?"

"I had been accepted to an art school in New York. After college, I moved to Paris and was a curator for one of the national museums until my father had a heart attack. I came home to help my parents. I volunteered for the mounted patrol and decided I really liked serving my community."

"And now you're a deputy."

"Yep. It's funny how life's twists and turns take us places we never expect. Who knows? If Daniel had made a different choice that night, I might not have gone so far away to school."

Simone was glad it would work out for the two deputies.

How would things turn out for her and Ian? Could there be a future for them? What would that even look like?

They arrived at the hospital and parked near the entrance. She fell into step with Ian. In the ICU, they found Nick, Kaitlyn and Mike at the nurses' station. Their frantic expressions didn't bode well.

Nick rushed to Ian, looking haggard. "I'm so glad you're alive."

Ian hugged his brother. "Me, too. I need to speak with Dad."

Nick stepped back and ran a hand through his dark hair. "He's gone."

Simone's heart stalled. Beside her, Ian staggered. She slid her arms around him. He leaned heavily on her.

"I'm too late," he said, his voice breaking.

Her heart ached for him, for all of them.

Ian's heart splintered. Grief, sharp and painful, sliced through him, leaving him raw. Marcus had won, after all. He'd had his father killed.

Kaitlyn nudged Nick aside. "No, it's not what you think. Your father has been moved."

The word reverberated through his brain. "Moved?"

"He's alive." Simone gave him a squeeze, drawing his gaze.

He nodded, picking up the pieces of his heart and putting them back together. "What floor is he on now?"

"You misunderstand," Kaitlyn said. "We just arrived and discovered that Nurse Janice arranged for Patrick to be taken to a rehab center on the outskirts of town."

Anxious to find his father, Ian said, "You have to find Nurse Janice. She's working with Marcus. We need to go to the rehab center."

"Oh, no. That's not good. I'll give them a call to verify he's there," Kaitlyn said. "And if so, let them know we're on our way." She went to the nurses' station to make the call.

Simone looked at Mike. "How did Janice get past you?"

He had a hangdog look on his face. "The nurse slipped

me a mickey in a bottle of water. Next thing I know, I'm tied up in a closet."

"We found him in the janitorial room," Nick added.

"Janice has a son," Simone said. "Marcus was threatening to hurt the child."

"We need to locate the son," Alex said. "Make sure he's safe."

"I'm on it," Leslie said. "I'll get the nurse's home address and drive over there."

"Call Daniel and have him meet you," Alex said.

"Yes, sir." Leslie hurried away.

Kaitlyn hurried back. "He's not at the rehab center. They had no idea what I was talking about. They'd never heard of Nurse Janice or Patrick."

Worry gnawed at Ian. "Where could she have taken our father?"

The worry in Alex's eyes ratcheted up Ian's anxiety. "I promise you, I will find him. But you need to go home. Shower, eat and get some rest."

"I'll go with you, Alex," Kaitlyn volunteered.

"No," Alex said. "You go with your family. Keep them safe. I'll meet up with Daniel and Leslie and call Chase in."

Frustrated, Ian let Simone lead him out of the hospital.

The drive up the mountain in another of the Delaney vehicles was quiet. Nick and Kaitlyn in front while Ian and Simone sat in the back. Ian's mind raced in circles with horrible scenarios. Was Nurse Janice keeping his father alive for the unknown boss—this KC or Casey person? Who was it and why did they want them dead?

When they arrived at the house, Simone touched Ian's arm. "Go clean up. You'll think more clearly after a hot shower and a change of clothes." She looked down at herself. "We're covered in ash. And we both stink."

He couldn't argue with her assessment.

An hour later, showered, shaved and dressed in fresh slacks and a button-down shirt, Ian entered his father's office. Alone for the moment with the clawing anxiety of not knowing where his father was or why someone was trying to hurt his family, he stared at the room. His eyes roamed over the wall of books, the credenza with all his father's files and the large mahogany desk with drawers. Could the answer to all of Ian's questions be in this room?

Awareness of Simone's presence skimmed over Ian. He turned to find her walking toward him, wearing the yoga pants and long-sleeved shirt she'd worn when they'd sparred. A sense of calm descended over him, as if having her near was an elixir to his angst. She'd let her hair down, the long waves cascading over her shoulders. He longed to feel her hair slide through his fingers. To kiss her again and forget all of this mayhem. But giving in to his feelings for Simone would not help him find his father. That had to be his priority.

Later he could examine how deeply he felt for this incredible woman who had unexpectedly entered his life. With effort, he turned away and strode to the desk. "There has to be answers here."

He sat in his father's chair and, opening the top drawer, searched through the contents without any success. Frustrated, he grasped the edges of the drawer, lifted it to release it from the track, and pulled it out. He then dumped everything onto the floor. He did the same with the rest of the drawers, figuring it would be easier to sift through the items and papers and whatnot in a larger space.

Simone moved to his side, placing her hand on his shoulder. "Creating more chaos is not going to help the situation."

He held her gaze, seeing the mess from her perspective. "But it'll make me feel better." Though it didn't really. He sat back in the chair and took her hand in his.

"I'm sorry you're going through this," she said softly.

He lifted her hand and kissed her knuckles. "I'm glad you're here with me."

Nick and Kaitlyn, holding Rosie against her shoulder, entered the room. They said nothing but stared at them. Ian saw the quirk of Nick's eyebrow and Kaitlyn's speculative gleam but didn't care. Simone tugged her hand away and stepped back. He wanted to draw her in but decided it was best to forge ahead. He waved his hand at the spilled drawers. "Help me look for answers."

Without commenting on what they'd no doubt seen, Nick joined Ian in methodically scrutinizing the contents on the floor. Kaitlyn laid the sleeping child on the leather couch and tucked throw pillows around her to prevent her from rolling off. Then Kaitlyn moved to help Simone tackle the credenza.

"We're looking for anything with the name Casey or the initials KC," Ian told Nick and Kaitlyn. He filled them in on what Joe had told him about this person being the mastermind behind the attacks.

When they'd gone through the contents of every drawer, every file, every book on the bookcase and had felt every inch of the furniture in the room, Ian's shoulders slumped. "There's nothing here."

He moved to stand before the floor-to-ceiling windows

overlooking the town of Bristle Township. In the distance, lights twinkled, reminding him of stars and diamonds. And Simone. His heart rate ticked up as he remembered their conversation about diamonds. He'd meant what he'd said. She should have diamonds.

"Let me get this straight," Kaitlyn said. "This Marcus character says your family somehow destroyed his? Or they're connected somehow?"

He turned to face his family. It wasn't lost on him that he included Simone in the label. "I don't know. I guess. Maybe he's just a raving lunatic." Ian ran a hand through his hair. "He was very cryptic. I don't really—"

A flash of something behind his eyes made him wince. Pain shot through his brain, but he couldn't hold on to the image.

Simone moved to his side and threaded her fingers through his. "Are you okay?"

With his free hand, he pinched the bridge of his nose. "I had a flash of what I think might've been the Dresden Group file. But…" He shook his head as the pain faded, along with any memory that had momentarily surfaced. "I don't know." He couldn't keep the frustration out of his voice.

"Okay. Don't push it. It will come in time," she said. She squeezed his hand then let go. "Let's think about this strategically."

He met her gaze. "What do you have in mind?"

"When I was leading investigations for the Detroit Police Department, whenever we would hit a roadblock, we would stop and start over," she said. "Go back to the beginning."

Grabbing onto her logic, he said, "We know it starts with me in my office. I asked Phyllis for the Dresden

Group file. She brought it to me. I had been looking at it." He frowned. "The next thing I know, I'm in the hospital."

Simone sat in the leather captain's chair and wrote on a piece of paper. "We know sometime after reviewing the file, you took the company jet from Boston to the top of the mountain here in Bristle Township, where you then fired up your helicopter and flew over the backside of the mountain." She scribbled notes on the paper.

"Where his helicopter crashed," Nick added.

Simone nodded and wrote that down.

"I was rescued and put in the hospital," Ian said. He remembered waking up to finding Simone standing at the foot of his bed, looking so fierce and beautiful. He never would have guessed how much she would come to mean to him.

"I called Trent Associates as soon as Alex told me the crash was caused by sabotage," Nick said.

"Someone tried to do you in while you were in the hospital," Kaitlyn pointed out.

"True." Simone tapped the pen on the desk. "How did they know you were alive and where to find you?"

"Good question," Nick said.

Ian shrugged.

"Then we returned to Boston," Simone said. "We went to your office. But the Dresden Group files were gone, wiped from your servers, and your office had been ransacked." She wrote that down.

"Who did you talk to while you were there?" Kaitlyn asked. "How many people knew you were alive?"

Ian groaned. "Everyone knew. I talked to the security guard. He'd already heard I was alive. Of course, Phyllis knew. Kevin, in the technology department, and Kathleen, the CFO. As well as every employee along the way."

"That's a lot of people," Kaitlyn said. "But I would hazard a very strong suspicion that someone in that building is our suspect."

"Which would explain why the men who shot at us knew when you were leaving the building." Simone wrote that down. "Yet we made it to the safe house."

"But how did they know we were on the way to the airport?" Ian asked.

From the doorway to the office, Mike said, "We filed a flight plan."

"That explains why there were men waiting in Bristle Township for us," Ian said.

"The attacks on the way to the airport most likely were from someone hacking into Ian's phone," Simone said. "We managed to get out of Boston and make it here."

"But once you were at the estate," Kaitlyn said as she picked up a sleepy Rosie and held her close, "our suspect knew the only way you would leave the house was if you thought something was wrong with Patrick, so they had Nurse Janice call you."

"Wait a second," Simone said, pointing the pen at Ian. "We forgot something."

"Did we?"

"Your safe-deposit box," she said. "Somebody used your name at the bank and cleaned it out."

Confused, Ian said, "But I already told you there was nothing inside the box worth killing over."

"Let's go through what you remember was in there," Simone suggested.

He moved to hitch his hip onto the edge of the desk. "A copy of my will, Dad's and Nick's. A few pieces of our mother's jewelry. Copies of the deeds to this house and my apartment in Boston. And copies of the deeds to our properties in Ireland and the UK."

"Since this seems to center around your father, could there be something in his will?" Simone asked.

Meeting her gaze, he said, "The original is with the family lawyer."

"There's a copy of Patrick's will in the safe upstairs in the panic room," Kaitlyn offered.

Everybody looked at her.

Kaitlyn's gaze was on Nick. "Patrick told me about the will a few months ago, in case anything should happen to him."

"Let's go look at it," Nick suggested, putting his arm around her.

Simone fell into step with Ian as they made their way upstairs to the panic room built into the hallway.

Ian opened the safe with the combination he'd memorized, then used his biometric thumbprint.

"Clever to have dual safeguards," Simone said.

"Oh, it's better than that," Kaitlyn said. "Each of us has our own numeric number plus our thumbprint."

"Our father's paranoid about security. He wanted a way to know who and when somebody opened the safe," Nick said.

"Yes, his need for security goes back to before coming to America," Ian said as he gathered all the contents of the safe and put them on the floor for them to look through.

"Our grandfather was just as paranoid," Nick noted.

"We only met him a couple times," Ian said. "Here's the will." He unfolded the document and skimmed the pages, handing them over for the others to read. When he reached the last page, aggravation had him gripping the paper. "Nothing in here about anyone with the name Casey or the initials KC."

Gently prying his fingers from the document and setting the paper aside, Simone said, "He could have added a codicil to his will."

Curling his fingers over hers, he said, "That's a good idea."

Twenty minutes later, Ian had the family lawyer, Jim McDonald, on speakerphone. Simone, Nick and Kaitlyn gathered close as Ian explained the situation.

"Your father didn't have me write up a codicil," Jim said.

"I noticed the current will is dated ten years ago," Simone said. "Was there a prior will?"

"Yes," Jim replied. "But it's invalid now."

"Okay, but do you have a copy of that one?" Ian asked, irritated and frustrated. Maybe the old will would give them some clues.

"No. Your father has the only copy."

"Could there have been a copy of the old will in your safe-deposit box?" Simone asked Ian.

"Possibly," Ian said with a sinking feeling. "Dad handed me an envelope and said it was his will. I didn't look at it."

"Jim, does the name Dresden ring any bells?" Nick asked.

There was a moment of hesitation then Jim said, "I only know that your company was once called D and D Holdings. I believe the other D was for Dresden. But your father changed the company name to Delaney Holdings back in the early seventies. Now, if you'll excuse me, I'll be going back to my evening." Jim hung up.

"Delaney and Dresden Holdings. That's the connection," Ian said. "We must find out everything we can about the Dresdens. Any information might be valuable at this point because it could lead us to my father." Where could he be?

FOURTEEN

The next morning, sunlight filtered in through the lace curtains of Simone's guest room at the Delaney estate. She'd spent a restless night dreaming of losing Ian in the smoke. A dream that had morphed into Ian with a bullet penetrating his chest and crimson-red blood staining his white dress shirt. Feelings of helplessness and despair tormented her until she'd awakened tired and cranky, wishing this whole ordeal was over yet bemoaning the fact that when it was over she would leave Ian behind.

Her heart had grown attached to him in unexpected ways. She shied away from thinking too deeply about how she felt. Letting herself become involved with him was a distraction and could compromise the success of this assignment.

Last night, after learning there was some sort of connection between the Delaney and Dresden families, Simone and Ian had spent several hours searching the World Wide Web for information on the Dresdens that could help them find his father. Their efforts had been in vain.

Simone put on the clothing Kaitlyn had loaned her. Western-style jeans that were a little snug and dropped to the tops of her shoes. She ended up rolling the pant legs to just above her ankles to make them capris. But the lightweight sweater in vibrant green fit perfectly. She toyed with the idea of putting her hair back up in a bun, but since she had no plans for them to leave the estate, she left it down, using her fingers to comb through the thick waves as she walked.

She hit the bottom stair, her gaze going to the library and zeroing in on Ian. He stood in front of the floor-to-ceiling bulletproof glass window, looking out over the vista. He'd changed into designer jeans and a blue V-neck sweater over a collared white shirt. When he turned to her, the pensive expression on his handsome face dissipated and he smiled, giving her heart a little jolt.

"I hope you slept well." He moved to gather her hands in his.

Staring into his dark eyes, she said, "Not really. Where's Mike?" Her associate had promised to stand guard through the night.

"I sent him to get some sleep. The grounds and house alarms are set. This place is a fortress," he assured her. "I'm more concerned over where my father is."

Empathy engulfed her. She could only imagine the ache of worry and anxiousness Ian and his family were suffering. She squeezed his hands. "I have confidence the sheriff will do everything possible to find your father."

"I trust Alex, but I want to do something," Ian said.

"I know you do," she said. "It's hard to be sidelined in an investigation. But we must be patient."

Simone hoped and prayed finding his father wouldn't end with the same result as when Beth had gone missing. But the situations were different. She had to put Beth out of her mind and stay focused on his father and Ian. She couldn't fail them.

Collins walked in. "Ian. Miss Walker. Would you like breakfast? Margaret made a feast."

"We would. Thank you." Ian tucked her hand in the crook of his arm and led her into the kitchen where the delicious scent of sausages and pancakes filled the air.

"Would you like to sit at the formal dining table?" Collins asked.

Simone made a face before she could stop herself.

Ian chuckled. "The countertop will do just fine." They sat side by side at the kitchen island. Margaret set a platter of fluffy pancakes and sausage links before them, along with plates and utensils.

A buzzing sound stalled Simone's breath. "What is that?"

"The front gate box," Ian said.

"I'll handle it," Collins said and walked out of the kitchen. Margaret left the kitchen, as well, leaving Ian and Simone alone to eat.

"Please, help yourself." Ian stabbed two pancakes and dropped them onto his plate.

Simone used a set of tongs to capture a couple of links and place them on her plate. "How will Collins 'handle' the front gate?"

"After the debacle last year with the men who were after Rosie, we had a new automatic delivery system installed. State-of-the-art technology. The postal worker, or messenger, puts the delivery in the box and it is delivered to the house. We don't have to let anyone in the gate."

Simone paused. "What if it's a bomb?"

Ian smiled. "We've seen to that safeguard, as well. All the packages are scanned as soon as they are put in the box."

Impressed, she said, "You've thought of everything."

"We have tried," he said.

They ate with gusto. A few minutes later, Collins walked in with a box and an envelope. He set both on the counter next to Ian. "Delivery service said these are from different parties."

"Thank you." Ian looked at the return addresses. "I was expecting this." He touched the box.

Collins retreated out the back door into the garden.

Ian picked up the envelope. "This is from Kathleen."

"The CFO?" She remembered the red-haired woman, the way she'd touched Ian with such familiarity. Did they have a thing going? A spurt of jealousy surprised her.

"Yes." He set it aside and opened the box. Inside were several burner phones. He took one out and handed it to Simone. "Untraceable and unhackable."

She grinned. "You really do think of everything."

He grinned and finished his breakfast.

"Are you going to open the envelope?" Simone's curiosity burned.

Ian wiped his mouth with his napkin and opened the envelope. He read the note then handed it to her.

Ian, darling,

I've been trying to reach you with no success. Has something happened to your cell phone? I've also been unable to reach your father. I have important documents and I need your signature. I am here in Bristle Township, staying at the Bristle Hotel. Room 262. Please get in touch with me at your earliest convenience.

Love, Kathleen XXOO

Simone hitched an eyebrow. "Does she always sign her missives to you with love and x's and o's?"

Ian shoved the note back into the envelope. "Sometimes. There's nothing going on between us, I promise you."

Simone held up her hand. "You don't have to explain yourself to me. I'm just the hired security." The words hurt more than she wanted to admit.

He took her hand and turned her palm up. Very gently, while maintaining eye contact, he kissed her palm.

A shiver coursed through her and her breath caught in her throat.

"Simone Walker, you are much more than just the hired security."

Her heart pounded in her chest. What was he saying? Did he feel the same pull of attraction and affection that she did?

The clearing of a throat had them jerking apart. She turned to find Nick with Rosie in his arms.

"I see breakfast is served," he said with a knowing grin.

"Where's Kaitlyn?" Simone asked, trying to cover the embarrassed heat creeping up her neck and settling in her cheeks.

Nick frowned. "She's got it in her head that she has to go to work today. I told her she needed to stay here, but she's insisting."

Ian stood. "Then we're going into town with her, so I can talk to Kathleen at the hotel."

A protest rose within Simone, but something in her expression must have given her imminent objection away because Ian cut her off. "Just because my life is in danger doesn't mean Delaney Holdings is on pause. I have business to attend to. I really would prefer not to have Kathleen come to the house."

So would Simone.

Ian reached into the box, pulled out the new burner phones, then proceeded to program each with the same numbers so they were all connected. "There's one for Mike. I'll give one to Kaitlyn." Ian pointed to the box. "Nick, there's one for you, too."

"Cool," Nick said, setting Rosie in her highchair.

"I'll grab my coat," Ian said. "And meet you and Mike outside."

Simone nodded and hurried down the hall to wake Mike. Within ten minutes, they were rolling out the gate of the estate with Mike driving the rented SUV they'd driven from Denver and Kaitlyn following them in a big pickup.

While Kaitlyn went to the sheriff's department, Mike parked the SUV in front of the hotel.

He stayed in the lobby, and Simone escorted Ian to the second floor. When the doors of the elevator opened, she stepped out first, making sure the hallway was clear. Then she waved him forward. They made their way to room 262. Tucking Ian behind her, she knocked.

The click of the door unlocking made Simone tense. Then it swung open. After a heartbeat, Simone stepped into the doorway and found herself face-to-face with Kathleen O'Connell. The redhead wore a black pencil skirt and a cream-colored blouse. The woman's bright smile faded to a frown. "I asked Ian to come, not his girlfriend."

"I'm here." Ian moved to Simone's side and put a hand around her waist, his fingers lightly resting on her hip.

The familiarity that she wouldn't allow from anyone else felt right from Ian.

Kathleen's gaze narrowed and her scowl deepened before she turned on her heels and walked into the suite's living area. Simone closed the door behind her as she and Ian followed Kathleen.

Kathleen stopped in the middle of the room and faced them, her gaze on Ian. "I didn't expect you to bring her."

Obviously. Judging from the bottle of champagne and two glasses sitting on the coffee table, she'd planned on having a cozy time alone with Ian. Simone wasn't at all regretful for thwarting the other woman's plans. Also on the table were a stack of papers and a pen. The reason they were there.

Kathleen waved a hand at the table. "All the papers are there for you to sign. I put sticky notes where your signature is required. It shouldn't take you long and you can be on your way, then I return to Boston."

"It won't be as simple or as quick as you think," Ian told her.

The woman's eyes widened. "And why not?"

He sat on the couch. "I need to read these documents to know what I'm signing."

Kathleen rolled her eyes. "No, you don't. Is your father around? I would have him sign these, but I can't locate him. Where is he?"

Ian's gaze shot to Simone. She shook her head. Kathleen didn't need to know that Patrick Delaney was missing.

"He's not available." Ian picked up the first document and gave it his attention.

Kathleen narrowed a glare on Simone then turned her focus on Ian. "Has your memory returned?"

Without looking up from the document in his hand, he said, "No, it has not. I'm still missing a week of my life."

Simone noticed the subtle way Kathleen's shoulders relaxed. She had been afraid he'd remembered something.

Interesting. Unease slithered over Simone. She stuck her hand in her pocket and fingered her burner phone. Something wasn't right here. Turning in the direction of the minibar where a fruit and cheese platter lay beside little plates, she pretended to busy herself getting food while she pressed the number Ian had programmed into the phone for Mike's phone and left the line open so he could hear what was going on.

When Simone turned back around, Kathleen had taken the seat next to Ian and put her hand on his shoulder, sliding her fingers down to his hand. "Ian, these are standard forms updating information for the audit I've been doing after the security breach. You have so much on your plate right now. How is the investigation into who is trying to kill you going, by the way?"

"The police have made some headway," Simone said, drawing Kathleen's gaze.

There was a flash of anger in the woman's eyes before she schooled her features. "Really? That's good." Kathleen returned her attention to Ian. "Please, if you could sign where I've indicated." She placed a hand over the documents before he could lift another. With her other hand, she fanned the bottom of the stack so he could see all the colorful sticky notes. "Just start at the back of the pile and work your way forward, signing as you go. That would be the most expedient."

Ian grabbed the papers from beneath her hand. "Kathleen, I am going to read each document."

Her jaw tightened and then she stood and moved to the window, but not before darting a glance over her shoulder toward the closed bedroom door.

Simone followed her gaze. Was somebody in there?

Slowly, she set down the plate of fruit and cheese she hadn't yet touched. "Do you mind if I use your restroom?" She put her hand on her weapon beneath her jacket and walked to the closed bedroom door.

"Wait!" Kathleen practically vaulted across the room. She grabbed the sleeve of Simone's jacket, halting her.

Simone released her hold on the grip of her gun and let her hand fall to her side.

"No. That's the bedroom. The bathroom is there." Kathleen pushed Simone toward the half-open door across the short hallway.

Simone pulled away from Kathleen. "On second thought, I'm good."

Kathleen stood there with her hands fisted.

Simone tilted her head and looked at the woman. "Are you okay, Kathleen? You look like you're about to go into shock. Is there something in the bedroom you don't want me to see?"

Kathleen jutted her chin. "I just didn't expect Ian to show up with you."

"So you said." Was Kathleen holding Patrick hostage in the bedroom? Or was the room staged for the seduction Kathleen had clearly planned?

A loud groan jerked Simone's attention to Ian. A hand braced on his forehead, he was doubled over a document held in his other hand. "I remember."

He lifted his head to look at Kathleen. The accusation in his eyes was both shocking and gratifying.

Kathleen was somehow involved in all this.

Simone, reaching behind her to rest her hand on the holstered weapon beneath her jacket, moved to stand in front of the minibar.

"I was signing papers in my office when I saw this." Ian held up the document.

From her position, Simone couldn't make out the details. "What is it?"

"This document signs over the title of the Dresden Group to someone named Kasey Dresden, with a K not C, along with the deeds to several properties in the UK and Ireland, including the plot of land outside Bristle Township." Ian slammed down the document and stood. "How could you do this?"

Kathleen rushed forward. "Please, Ian, just sign the papers so that no one else——"

The bedroom door swung open and a tall, broad-shouldered man with light red hair stepped out, holding an AK-47 aimed at Simone's chest.

Simone made a split-second decision to not draw on the man. Instead, she let her hand fall away from her weapon and gripped the minibar. "You have an assault rifle."

She sent up a prayer that Mike was listening and that this man didn't decide to spray the room with bullets.

"And I'm not afraid to use it," he said in a thick brogue. "Put your hands up." His glare jumped to Kathleen. "You're just as much of an idiot as our little brother."

Kathleen bridled. "I had it handled. If you had just given me more time. You shouldn't even be here."

"I had to be here because you and Marcus weren't getting the job done!" Kasey yelled.

Simone took the opportunity as the two argued to rush to Ian. Playing up the persona of his girlfriend, she launched herself into his arms, shielding him with her body. When he tried to reverse their positions, she stepped on his toes. She had to keep him safe from the siblings.

She only hoped help arrived before it was too late.

Ian's toes smarted, and he tightened his arms around Simone as alarm punctuated every breath in his body. He remembered now what had sent him into the forest. He'd also seen shipping manifests that routed unnamed cargo to Bristle Township. He'd known something was going on and had needed to check it out before calling in the authorities. Mostly, he'd been afraid his father was up to some sort of shenanigans, like he'd done with the treasure hunt. Ian now felt confident his father wasn't involved. Kathleen had betrayed their family. Why?

Keeping his eyes on the man with the firepower, Ian asked, "Who are you?"

"Kat, tell him who I am."

Kathleen made a face. "Don't call me that." With a sigh, she turned to Ian. "This is my fraternal twin brother, Kasey."

Shock ran through Ian. "Twins. And Marcus is your little brother. You told me you didn't have any family."

She shrugged.

"Does my father know?"

"Of course he knows," Kasey said. "We're here because of him."

Ian's gaze bounced between the twins. "What does that even mean?"

Kathleen sank onto a chair. Her shoulders slumped.

"You're not in a position to be asking questions,"

Kasey said. "You need to sign those documents, or I'll kill your father."

Anger reared through Ian. "You have my father. Is he here?"

"Not here," Kasey said. "But close."

"What makes you think I believe you?"

Simone tightened her hold on him, drawing his look. The expression in her eyes was clear: don't antagonize the man. Ian took a breath. He focused on Kathleen. "Explain to me what's going on. Why would you betray us like this?"

The woman laughed, the brittle sound raising the hairs on his neck.

"Why? Because your father betrayed our family," she said. "Our grandfathers were in business together. They formed D and D Holdings. Our fathers were best friends. They came up through the ranks of the IRA together."

Ian's knees buckled. Simone held him upright. "No. My father and my grandfather would not—"

"But they were. Our fathers took over the company business after our grandfathers retired." Kathleen shot her brother a look. "But then our mother was diagnosed with cancer and your father bought my father out."

Ian's mind spun. This was all news to him. His father had never breathed a word of a partner.

"And then Patrick decided to leave Ireland and take everything our family had helped build to America," Kasey said.

"None of this makes any sense," Ian said. "If what you're saying is true, then where's the betrayal? My father acted honorably and paid your father for his half of the company."

Kathleen's lip curled. "My father used the money to pay for our mother's doctor bills."

"I'm sorry for your loss, but I still don't understand."

Kathleen stood, her fists clenched. "With what money was left over, our father bought a chain of markets throughout Northern Ireland and the Republic of Ireland."

"It seems like a wise investment," Ian said. "But I still don't see what this has to do with my family."

"Of course you don't. You're the golden children, you and your brother. Insulated from all the ugliness. The poverty… The markets barely turned enough of a profit for us to survive. I married young and, unfortunately, Finn O'Connell died unexpectedly, leaving me with enough money to go to university."

That part Ian had heard. "And my father offered you a job."

"Yes. I worked my way up to CFO. With one goal in mind. To take down the great Delaneys."

Ian met Simone's gaze, saw his own surprise reflected there. Kathleen's twisted logic was going to get him and Simone killed.

The woman began to pace. "When our father died, we discovered he didn't own the Dresden Group, as he'd told us. The great Patrick Delaney had taken pity on our father and given him the chain of stores to run but had retained ownership." She stopped and faced Ian. "For years I've been funneling money into the group so that Kasey, Marcus and I would not have to struggle. But then you had to go and ruin everything."

"That's why you have been trying to kill Ian," Simone said.

"If only Marcus had done the job he'd been sent here to do," Kasey said.

Kathleen grabbed the paperwork from the floor where it had fallen and held up the pen. "Just sign the documents and we can get out of here."

"Where's my father?" Ian said. "I'll sign those papers if you take me to my father."

Kathleen grabbed her purse from where it hung on the back of a chair and jammed the papers into it. "Fine." She turned to her brother. "Let's take him and his girlfriend to see Patrick Delaney one last time."

Draping a jacket over the AK-47, Kasey gestured for Simone and Ian to move. They had no choice but to follow Kathleen out of the room and down the hotel staircase to the rear parking lot door.

"I didn't know there were stairs that led to the back of the hotel," Simone commented as they were marched toward a parked minivan.

Ian slanted her a confused glance. Why would that matter at a time like this?

They were shoved into the minivan.

Kathleen took the driver's seat while her twin settled in the passenger seat and set the assault rifle on his lap then pulled a handgun from the glove box, which he waved at them. "Don't think I won't use this."

After a few minutes, Simone reached for Ian's hand and gave it a squeeze. "Why are we heading south? Whose blue minivan is this?"

Her questions earned her a scathing scowl from Kasey. "Be quiet."

Ian willed Simone not to do anything to get herself hurt, then sent up a prayer that they would get out of this situation alive.

FIFTEEN

Sitting next to Ian in the minivan's middle row of seats, Simone was relieved she had claimed to be a close friend of Ian's when she'd first met Kathleen in his Boston office. And thankful Kasey must not consider her a threat because he hadn't searched her. If he'd found her weapon or the phone in her pocket with an open connection to Mike, who knew what would've happened?

With Kasey in the front passenger seat, the AK-47 lying across his lap with the business end aimed at her and Ian, and a handgun in his hand, Kathleen drove away from town as if familiar with their destination.

Simone fought the urge to swivel in her seat to look out the back window to see if Mike was following. She nudged Ian with her elbow, gaining his attention. She pulled the phone out of her pocket just high enough for him to see that the line was open and Mike was listening. His eyes widened with understanding.

The minivan turned down a gravel road. "Why are we turning onto a no-name road off the highway? Where are you taking us?" With little effort, Simone infused a fearful note into her voice. Up ahead, a dilapidated farmhouse came into view. "That farm looks abandoned.

We're on the south side of Bristle Township, aren't we? Who lives here?"

"You ask a lot of questions," Kasey said. "I don't like it. Stop talking."

Ian put his hand over hers. The simple gesture created havoc with her senses. She curled her fingers around his, hanging on in a way that made her aware of how much she'd come to love this brave and wonderful man. "You'll have to excuse my girlfriend. She's the curious sort."

Leaning into him, she said, "Sorry, darling. But I'm scared."

She would be careful until she got a lay of the land and learned that Patrick Delaney was really alive. Then she could plan a way out of this for them all. But, for now, she needed to bide her time by continuing to play the girlfriend role. She didn't want to give Kasey or Kathleen any reason to eliminate her from the equation. However, she couldn't wait to neutralize the threat the twins posed to Ian and his family.

The minivan pulled up in front of the farmhouse. Kasey handed Kathleen the handgun, then climbed out and yanked open the sliding side door, gesturing for them to follow him. Kathleen had gone on ahead, opening the farmhouse door.

Simone carefully stepped out and moved aside for Ian to join her. She shielded her eyes against the midmorning sun. Signs of the forest fire that had started at the militia camp marred the landscape. "We aren't far from where Marcus's training camp was located."

Kasey whirled on her. "My training camp. Our little brother wasn't smart enough to come up with the plan to train our men here. That was me." He pushed Ian. "In the house."

They climbed the rickety stairs to the front door. Simone and Ian entered the dimly lit house. It took a moment for Simone's eyes to adjust. Patrick Delaney lay on a hospital bed in the middle of the living room. Ian rushed to his father's side. Nurse Janice stood nearby. A young boy, Simone guessed was the nurse's son, lay curled up on the couch. Another man with a handgun stood in the corner.

"How is my father?" Ian asked Nurse Janice.

The woman darted a frantic gaze at Kasey. "He's holding his own for now." Her voice held a tremor. "But he needs to be on oxygen. His breathing is labored."

Kathleen withdrew the papers from her purse and offered the pen to Ian. "You've seen your father. Now sign these. Then you all can go on your way."

"Is that true? You'll let us leave here if Ian does as you've asked?" Simone stood between the thug in the corner and Kasey, yet close enough to Ian that she could shove him out of the way if she needed to.

"Of course it's true," Kathleen snapped, hitching her purse higher on her shoulder.

Simone shook her head. "I don't believe you."

"What does it matter what you believe?" Kathleen said. She pushed the papers into Ian's chest. "Sign them."

Simone hoped that with Kathleen so close to Ian, no one would attempt to shoot him. Unless, of course, Kasey wanted to get rid of his sister, too. Somehow, she didn't think it would be a hardship for the man. There didn't seem to be much love lost between the siblings.

Simone looked at Kasey. "You have no intention of letting any of us go. How do you plan to get out of Bristle Township? Or Colorado, for that matter?"

"No one's going to think twice about a family in a minivan," Kasey said.

Dread gripped Simone's gut. "You plan to take Janice's son with you?"

Janice gasped. "You promised you wouldn't hurt us." She hurried to the couch and gathered her son close.

"Yeah, yeah," Kasey said. "Words are cheap."

A loud voice from outside the house yelled, "This is the ATF. You're surrounded. Come out with your hands in the air."

Though Simone should feel relief that the cavalry had arrived, the tension in the house increased. Kasey ran to the window and peered out. The thug joined him.

Assuming Mike, or the ATF agent in charge, was still listening via the open line of the phone in her pocket, Simone said, "Why are you two standing by the window? Is your plan to shoot your way out? It would be suicide."

Desperation etched on her face, Kathleen clutched at Ian. "Just sign these now."

Ian pushed her away from him. "I will do no such thing."

Kasey faced the room and aimed the AK-47 at Ian. "Then you're a dead man."

"Don't shoot," Simone said, hopefully alerting the agents outside.

"Let Janice and her son go," Ian said. "They aren't a part of this."

"It would be a show of good faith," Simone said. "If you want to get out of here alive, you need to give the ATF something."

"And my girlfriend," Ian insisted. "She's not a part of your plan. Let her go."

Simone gritted her teeth. "I'm not leaving you, Ian, darling. You should know that."

A pained look crossed Ian's face. But he turned to Kathleen. "Please, just let my girlfriend go. I'll do as you ask. I'll sign the papers."

"Enough of this!" Kasey yelled. "You'll do as Kat asked or you and your father will both die right here, right now. I don't mind taking my revenge in the form of your deaths." To the thug who moved forward, he said, "Tie her and those two up. We'll use them to get out of here."

The creak of a footstep on the porch drew Kasey's attention.

As Kasey's man moved toward Simone, Ian sprang into action. He shoved Kathleen aside and leg-swept the thug, sending him crashing to the floor. Then Ian jumped on the guy's back and secured him with a headlock.

Seizing the opportunity, Simone withdrew her weapon and aimed at Kasey, firing just as the man's finger moved to the trigger of the assault rifle. Simone's bullet lodged itself into Kasey's thigh and the man went down, his weapon clattering to the floor.

Clutching his leg, Kasey bellowed. "Oww. You shot me."

"Two down," Simone stated aloud. She kicked the rifle aside and scooped up the handgun the thug had dropped.

Then she turned and froze.

Kathleen had the handgun Kasey had given her pressed to Patrick's temple. "So the girlfriend is more than she seems. Are you ATF?"

Ignoring the question, Simone trained one of the handguns she held at Kathleen while keeping the other aimed squarely on the woman's brother.

"Kathleen has a weapon on Patrick," she said aloud for Mike's benefit. "Ian, come to me."

Ian held up his hands and moved off the now unconscious guard. He took a step toward Kathleen, but she pivoted and grabbed his arm, yanked him closer, shifting the barrel of the gun into his ribs. Anger flashed in Ian's eyes as his body visibly tensed. Had he planned to try to take the gun from the woman?

"She has her finger on the trigger," Simone told him and everyone listening. She held his gaze. "Don't make any sudden moves."

Determination etched his features. He broke eye contact with Simone to stare at Kathleen. "What's the plan here, Kathleen? You kill my father, then us, and leave a trail of bodies? You'll never get what you want."

Kathleen sneered at him. "It's too late for what I want. If you'd just done as I'd asked and signed the papers, none of this would've happened. But now revenge is my only recourse for making our family suffer."

"Your only way out of here is with me," Ian said.

"Uh, no." Simone moved closer. "Ian, you're not leaving with her. Kathleen, put the gun down."

"Kathleen, take me hostage," Ian said. "The agents will let us leave and then you can have whatever money is in the Dresden Group and disappear."

Simone wanted to scream with frustration. Why did he always insist on being in control and doing things his way? "Don't do this. Don't try to be a hero."

"I trust you to have my back." His gaze caressed her, the soft light in his dark eyes sending her pulse jumping. "I love you."

Simone's heart jolted. He didn't mean it. Those words were just part of their act. Her heart beating in her throat, an urge to tell him that she loved him rose, but she bit the words back. She needed to stay focused on keeping Ian and his father alive.

"Isn't that so sweet? Telling your cop girlfriend you love her." Kathleen shuffled Ian toward the door. "Tell everyone to back off." Her gaze bore into Simone. "If you or anyone tries to stop us, I will shoot him. I've nothing to lose."

"Do as she says, Simone," Ian said. "Let us walk out of here, away from my father."

Though she understood his need to protect his father, Simone hated that he would do so at his own expense. If she let him make this choice and it went bad, resulting in him ending up dead, she didn't think she could survive.

Still writhing in pain, clutching at the bullet wound in his leg, Kasey asked, "Sister, what about me?"

Kathleen looked at him with derision. "You're on your own, brother. Don't think I know you wouldn't sacrifice me if you had the chance, just as you did Marcus."

Kathleen pushed Ian toward the door.

Ian twisted to meet Simone's gaze. "Keep my father safe. I'm trusting you to have my back."

"Ugh. Move it." Kathleen yanked open the door and shoved Ian through the opening.

"We're coming out," Ian shouted. "Don't shoot."

Frustration crawling up her spine, Simone wanted to follow but a scraping noise drew her attention. Kasey was crawling his way toward the AK-47. "Oh, no, you don't." She beat him to the rifle.

She could only pray that Joe and the rest of them wouldn't allow Kathleen to take Ian away.

Heavy footsteps coming from the back of the house had Simone whirling to identify the intruders.

Mike stepped out from the kitchen. Two ATF agents were close on his heels.

"Thought you might need a hand." He held up zip ties.

"Yes." Together they quickly bound Kasey and his thug.

Simone looked at Janice. "Tend to his wound."

The nurse made a face but nodded and hurried to put pressure on Kasey's injured leg.

"You good here?" Simone asked Mike.

"Go," he said. "Protect Ian."

Yes, she would, and then she was going to give the man a piece of her mind.

She hurried out the back door and rounded the house, pausing at the corner. Kathleen and Ian stood in the middle of the driveway, facing at least a dozen ATF agents and the sheriff and his deputies. Simone caught Joe's eye and gestured toward Kathleen. He gave a subtle nod.

In a loud voice, Joe said, "Mrs. O'Connell, what is it you need?"

Simone used the distraction Joe provided to slowly make her way toward Kathleen and Ian, careful to tread lightly over the gravel drive.

"We're getting in the minivan," Kathleen said in a loud voice. After rooting around in her purse with her free hand for her keys, she said, "Clear a path and have a plane waiting at the airport to take me anywhere I want to go."

"Release your hostage," Joe said. "Then we'll let you leave."

"You think me a fool?" Kathleen's voice seethed with

anger. "I won't hesitate to shoot him if anyone tries to stop us."

Joe made a motion with his hand for his agents to back up. "Fine. But just so you know, there will be no safe place for you."

"Move," Kathleen said to Ian, shoving him forward a step.

Simone closed the distance until she was directly behind Kathleen. With a gun in each hand, Simone pressed the barrel of one to the back of Kathleen's head and the other low on her spine. "Drop your weapon."

Kathleen stiffened. "I'll shoot him."

"And I'll shoot you," Simone hissed into her ear, pressing the gun barrel harder into Kathleen's spine.

With a frustrated growl, Kathleen dropped her weapon. Ian jerked away from her and scooped the gun up, quickly handing the piece to Joe.

The sheriff moved in to handcuff Kathleen and take her into custody. Two paramedics rushed past to tend to Kasey and Patrick Delaney. The thug had come to and was escorted out in handcuffs. Nurse Janice and her son were brought out, as well. A woman who identified herself as Cara Colson from Child Protective Services took custody of Janice's son. Janice was read her rights and escorted away to a waiting vehicle.

Ian hugged Simone and breathed into her hair, "I knew you'd have my back."

Simone pushed him away as anger tore through her. "Do you know how reckless and dangerous that was? You could have been seriously injured or killed, not to mention putting everyone's life in jeopardy."

He grimaced. "I had to protect my father and you."

"No. It was my job to protect you."

"You did." Ian reached for her hands. "You protected me and everyone else. I am beyond grateful."

A car screeching to a halt drew their attention.

Nick and Kaitlyn jumped out of a sheriff's department vehicle and ran toward the house.

Simone shifted her gaze back to Ian and her heart melted. It was hard to stay mad at him when he was looking at her with such tenderness. "Go see to your family. I need to give my statement. You'll have to give yours, too."

He lifted her hand to his lips and pressed a kiss to her knuckles. "Don't leave without talking to me first."

Did he mean leave the scene? Or leave town?

Ian and his family were safe. It was time for Simone to return to Boston, yet everything inside her cried out with protest. She wanted to stay with Ian. To tell him she loved him. To forge a future together.

But she wasn't sure if his feelings for her were real. And she was afraid to ask because it would hurt too much if she learned it was just part of the charade.

As much as the words pained her to say, she had no choice. "I can't make you any promises."

Ian wanted to stop Simone from walking away. He wanted to tell her he'd meant what he'd said. He loved her. But with everyone watching, and her so angry, he decided the best course of action would be to wait. He hurried back into the old farmhouse to find Kaitlyn and Nick gushing over Patrick, who was wide awake and sitting up with an oxygen mask over his face. Ian nodded to Mike, who ushered the paramedics out the door, leaving the family alone for the moment.

Ian frowned with confusion. "You're awake?"

Patrick removed the mask. "Yes. I've been awake for a while, but it seemed prudent not to let those kids know."

"You knew who was trying to kill me this whole time?" Ian couldn't keep the hurt from his voice.

"No, Ian, I didn't know," Patrick insisted. He placed the oxygen mask to his face and took several breaths before continuing. "I only realized the twins were involved when I woke up here. I gave Kathleen the job, but never suspected the ill will she harbored. Her father was once my best friend."

"They are more than involved." Ian related everything Kathleen had told him about their family's connection.

"No way," Nick said. "You and Grandfather were part of the IRA?"

"It was a long time ago, in a different life," Patrick said. "I promise you I was never a part of the violence."

"Why didn't you ever tell us about the Dresdens?" Ian asked, taking his father's hand. "You gave Kathleen a job but never mentioned her brothers or your close association with her father."

"I didn't want questions about my past. Your mother and I wanted a clean slate here in America," Patrick said. "But I suppose you deserve to know."

He took in more oxygen before saying, "As a teen, I was an errand boy for the IRA, but my mother sent me to live with her cousins in England. I was there for most of my twenties and part of my thirties. I returned to Ireland and started D and D Holdings with Seamus Dresden. Then I met your mother, and it changed my life."

Just as meeting Simone had changed Ian's life. He couldn't imagine living without her by his side. He needed to go find her. To tell her—

"Excuse me." Joe stepped into the living room, diverting Ian's thoughts. "Ian, we need your statement." His gaze zeroed in on Patrick. "And yours, Mr. Delaney."

"I'm ready to get out of here," said Patrick, lying back with the oxygen mask once more over his face. The paramedics returned, wheeled him out of the farmhouse, and put him in the back of an ambulance.

It was several hours later before Ian returned to the estate. His father was once again in the hospital, but the doctors were confident he would be released in a day or two when his levels stabilized.

Ian was exhausted, but he was anxious to find Simone to secure their future together. He prayed she returned the depth of his feelings for her. If not, then he would do all in his power to convince her they belonged together. They made a great team but, more important, he loved her with every fiber of his being. He knew full well the risk of opening his heart to Simone, but not allowing her in would be more damaging.

She and Mike had left the sheriff's office earlier, but she'd not said a word to him since the farmhouse. Ian found Simone in the guest room, packing. Her actions were jerky, as if fighting with her emotions. She was so beautiful. He drank in the sight, committing every detail to memory. Her dark hair, pulled back into a low ponytail, swished every time she moved. Her lips were pressed into a thin line. He wanted to see her smile, to hear her laugh. To see joy in her eyes.

He remained rooted in the open doorway, words forming and then dying on his lips. He didn't know how to do this. Sudden insecurity plagued him. He'd never laid his emotions bare before. Would she ease the longing in his heart? Or would he have to resort to groveling at her feet in the hope that she could love him in return?

"Are you just going to stand there not saying anything?" she asked as she zipped up her duffel bag.

There was no mistaking the edge to her voice. "You're still angry with me."

"I'm angry with myself," she said. "I need to rethink my line of work, because I didn't do a very good job protecting you."

"What?" He strode across the room and took hold of her biceps, turning her to face him. The self-recrimination in her eyes made him hurt. "You did everything you were supposed to and more. My family is safe because of you."

"But it could have gone so wrong," she insisted, her intent gaze boring into him.

The agony on her lovely face sliced at him worse than any knife could. "Simone, *could haves* don't count. We're all safe. And the people responsible have been arrested. You are the best at what you do. And I couldn't love you any more than I do right now."

She frowned and tucked in her chin. Not the reaction he was hoping for.

"You don't have to pretend anymore," she said.

"This isn't an act," he said. "And I wasn't acting at the farmhouse. I love you, Simone." The words felt so right. He twirled a lock of her hair around his finger. "I think I fell in love with you the first time I saw you standing over me in the hospital, looking so fierce and determined. My own warrior."

The disbelief in her eyes made him add, "But it was as I came to know you more that I discovered you're everything I am missing in my life."

"Ian—"

He held up a hand. "Let me finish, please. I've held everyone, at least those outside of my family, at a distance. Too afraid to let anyone in. Mostly because I'd seen how loving someone so much had broken my father when my mother died. I vowed long ago I would never go through that."

Her expression softened. She placed a hand over his heart. Her touch was light, but warm and sure. "I understand. Letting people in is risky. I haven't let anyone in because I was afraid of letting them down. Like I had with Beth."

"Hey, now—" he protested.

"I know," she interrupted. "She made her choice, and I have to accept that. But I can't forget how terrified I was—I am—of letting you down."

He covered her hand with his. "You haven't let me down. You have never let anyone down." He took a steadying breath and plunged ahead. "Please say you'll stay with me."

"I have to leave," she said.

Heartache speared him to the core. "Because you don't love me."

She made a distressed noise and tugged her hand from beneath his then wound both her hands around his neck. "No, silly. I do love you. That's why I need to go."

There was the joy he yearned to see in her eyes. Both elated and confused, he didn't know what to do. "I don't understand. You love me, but you need to leave me?"

"Yes, I love you. I don't know exactly when it happened, but somewhere along the way, I fell for you. Hard." Her fingers stroked the back of his neck, sending delicious shivers down his spine. "But I need to go talk to James in person. I don't know what working for Trent Associates from Colorado would look like."

"We can live in Boston in my apartment there and

visit Colorado," Ian said, his heart rate ticking up and his pulse jumping. She loved him! "Where we live is not a problem."

"You're okay with me being a bodyguard?"

He hesitated to think about that. She'd be off on dangerous missions, protecting people, just as she'd done for him. She was good at her job. And he couldn't ask her to give that up. She was a protector. It was in her nature. Sure, he'd worry and long for her to return to him. But there were no guarantees in life. He'd learned that over the past few days.

However, an idea formed. Something Kaitlyn had said stuck in his mind. "You know, Bristle County Sheriff's Department could use another deputy. Kaitlyn will be out on maternity leave soon, and who knows, she may not return to work. You'd be a great addition to the department. I can fly out to Boston when I need to."

She arched an eyebrow. "Something to consider."

He dropped his forehead to hers. "Honestly, you can do anything you want with your life as long as you include me in it."

"Good," she said.

The happiness in her voice made him grin.

"Boston for now," she said. "Then… I was thinking we could plan a camping trip for the spring."

He groaned. "Can we not do the woods for a while? How about a water excursion on a yacht built for two?"

She waggled her eyebrows. "Sounds romantic, if I don't get seasick."

He grinned. "Well, there's that. Maybe a short day trip to get you your sea legs."

"Sounds like a good first date."

"I want a lifetime of firsts," he said.

She drew back. "What are you saying?"

"I can't imagine a future without you," he said. "I want you in my life, forever and always. I know that, no matter what life throws at us, being with you for however long God deems, is worth everything to me. Whether in Boston or Bristle Township or some other place across the globe." He caressed her cheek. "Will you marry me as soon as possible? I don't want to wait. Even a few days is too long."

A delighted smile broke out over Simone's lovely face. "Yes, to a lifetime of firsts and lasts and everything in between. I don't want to wait, either."

His heart bursting with joy, he dipped his head and kissed her.

EPILOGUE

"A toast." Nick's voice rang out as he rose from his seat with his glass held high. Beside him, Kaitlyn cuddled their newborn baby boy to her shoulder and helped their daughter, Rosie, to hold on to a small plastic cup.

Sitting at the head table, Ian grinned at his brother, proud of the man he'd become. Ian had never dreamed that Nick would be a pillar of the community, a family man and Ian's best man.

Ian turned his gaze onto his lovely bride. She glowed. There was no other way for Ian to describe Simone's beauty and the joy emanating from her smile. Her elegant wedding dress hugged her curves, tasteful and demure, but, oh, so wonderful. Her dark hair spilled over her shoulders in thick waves that he couldn't wait to run his fingers through. Diamonds sparkled in the custommade piece around her neck and on her left hand as she lifted her crystal goblet and met his gaze. The love shining there made his chest swell with pride, love and joy.

All around them, their guests raised glasses and quieted.

Ian tore his eyes from his wife and took in the sea of smiling faces.

They'd intended to have a small, intimate wedding and reception with just their families in attendance, but somehow the guest list had grown until practically the whole town of Bristle Township, along with Simone's colleagues from Trent Associates who'd arrived in the Trent jet for the event, had filled the church and now sat at various round, linen-clad tables inside the Bristle Township Community Center's large event space.

Ian glanced at the sheriff's department table and met Alex Trevino's gaze. Alex's head dipped with an approving nod. Ian was gratified to have his friend and his family showing their support. Maya Trevino sat beside her husband, looking lovely in a peach-colored dress that did nothing to hide the growing mound of her expectant belly. Next to Maya sat Brady Gallo, Maya's young brother. The boy could hardly contain his excitement. Ever since Ian had asked him to be a part of the wedding party, Brady had researched all the ways a groomsman was to help the groom.

Also seated at the table were deputies Daniel Rawlings and Leslie Quinn. Ian had heard they'd become engaged and were planning on a wedding next month. Good thing Simone had accepted Alex's offer to come on board at the sheriff's department after she and Ian returned from their honeymoon. It would allow Daniel and Leslie to go on their own honeymoon without leaving the department shorthanded. Beside the happy couple sat Deputy Chase Fredrick and his wife, Ashley. She bounced an infant girl on her knee.

"Get on with it, boy," Patrick Delaney groused from his place at the table where he sat with Simone's family, who had flown in from Detroit.

Love for his father made Ian smile. A rumble of laughter swept through the room. His new in-laws were a huge blessing, as well. Simone's parents and brothers had welcomed him and the Delaney family into their fold.

"To my big brother and his beautiful wife." Nick's voice drew Ian's attention. "An Irish blessing." He cleared his throat. "'May the raindrops fall lightly on your brow. May the soft winds freshen your spirit. May the sunshine brighten your heart. May the burdens of the day rest lightly upon you. And may God enfold you in the mantle of His love…

"'May your troubles be less and your blessings be more. To all the days here and after, may they be filled with fond memories, happiness, and laughter galore.' Cheers!"

The crowd gathered to celebrate the marriage of Ian and Simone said in unison, "Cheers!"

Ian clinked his goblet to Simone's and stared into her eyes. "To us. Forever more."

She grinned. "I'm looking forward to the next two weeks."

He laughed. "Me, too."

They'd settled on a compromise for their honeymoon. A week camping in the Berkshire Forest of Massachusetts then a week of sailing the Atlantic on their new yacht. Simone had proved to have no trouble on the open seas and she was convinced he'd love being in the woods without the worry of gunmen and fires.

As long as they were together, he'd be content.

* * * * *

If you enjoyed this story, look for these other books by Terri Reed:

Buried Mountain Secrets
Secret Mountain Hideout
Christmas Protection Detail

Dear Reader,

I hope you enjoyed Ian Delaney and Simone Walker's story. When I decided to do Ian's book, I had no idea what chaos the world would be in while I labored to give him a happily-ever-after. I knew he needed a strong woman who would challenge him and soften his edges. Simone Walker came to mind. She was a secondary character in a series of books I wrote a few years back featuring bodyguards. I'd always intended to give her a book, but then life intervened with other stories. I'm glad I was able to finally give her the happily-ever-after she deserved, though it was hard fought as she protected Ian from the threat wanting to do him harm. In some ways, Ian and Simone were very much alike: both wanting to be in control, both used to doing things their way and both guarding their hearts. But, as always, love smoothed over their similarities and their differences, allowing them to enjoy all that love has to offer.

Until we meet again. May God bless you and keep you in His care.

COMING NEXT MONTH FROM
Love Inspired Suspense

DANGEROUS MOUNTAIN RESCUE
K-9 Search and Rescue • by Christy Barritt

Erin Lansing will search every inch of the mountains to find her teen daughter who has disappeared—even if someone is intent on stopping her at all costs. Teaming up with search-and-rescue K-9 handler Dillon Walker and his dog, Scout, might be her only chance at seeing her daughter again...and staying alive.

DEATH VALLEY DOUBLE CROSS
Desert Justice • by Dana Mentink

As family secrets surface, Pilar Jefferson must unravel the mystery of her supposedly deceased father in order to find her missing mother—and escape an assassin. But when her ex-fiancé, Austin Duke, gets pulled into the investigation, will she survive long enough for her to tell him the real reason she fled on their wedding day?

SMUGGLERS IN AMISH COUNTRY
by Debby Giusti

Tracking a robbery suspect forces Atlanta cop Marti Sommers to go undercover in an Amish community where the criminal is attacking delivery girls. When Luke Lehman's niece is threatened, Marti will have to partner with the former officer turned Amish guardian to save everyone they care about...including each other.

TEXAS COLD CASE THREAT
Quantico Profilers • by Jessica R. Patch

When a murderer sends her taunting letters, FBI behavioral analyst Chelsey Banks retreats to a friend's ranch—and interrupts the housekeeper being attacked. Learning it matches the MO of a cold-case serial killer, she'll need to work with her best friend, Texas Ranger Tack Holliday—unless one of the culprits gets her first.

SAFE HOUSE EXPOSED
by Darlene L. Turner

After a leak in the Canadian witness protection program exposes his sister-in-law and his niece, police constable Mason James races to protect them. But with a crime family hunting Emma and little Sierra, there's no safe place to hide...and nobody to trust.

TRACKING CONCEALED EVIDENCE
by Sharee Stover

Discovering Detective Shaylee Adler buried alive is only the first clue former forensic entomologist Jamie Dyer and cadaver dog Bugsy unearth. Together, they'll have to untangle the connections between Shaylee's missing sister, her senator brother-in-law and the person now hunting them all.

———————

LISCNM0122B

Get 4 FREE REWARDS!

We'll send you 2 FREE Books
plus 2 FREE Mystery Gifts.

Love Inspired Suspense books showcase how courage and optimism unite in stories of faith and love in the face of danger.

FREE Value Over $20

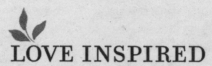